TARGET PRACTICE

Slocum quickly popped up and leveled his rifle while the last two Conrad boys reloaded. His eye caught a place where the brush was bent the wrong way, like somebody was back in there leaning on it, and he aimed low and just to the right of it.

He pulled the trigger.

Dread Conrad, the youngest and undoubtedly the meanest of the quartet, staggered from the brush on his knees, a bright red stain spreading on his chest and fell forward into the scrub onto his ugly bucktoothed face. He didn't move again.

"Arvil Conrad!" Slocum called. "You're all alone there, Arvil. Why don't you give up and make it easy on everybody?"

Arvil opened fire.

Just as Slocum's head cleared the top of the rock, Sam fired. Arvil's body fell backward, out into the clear. It twitched once, and then went still.

"Hoop-de-doodle!" said Sam. "I do believe we're each two for two there, Slocum."

DON'T MISS THESE
ALL-ACTION WESTERN SERIES
FROM THE BERKLEY PUBLISHING GROUP

THE GUNSMITH by J. R. Roberts
Clint Adams was a legend among lawmen, outlaws, and ladies. They called him . . . the Gunsmith.

LONGARM by Tabor Evans
The popular long-running series about Deputy U.S. Marshal Long—his life, his loves, his fight for justice.

SLOCUM by Jake Logan
Today's longest-running action Western. John Slocum rides a deadly trail of hot blood and cold steel.

BUSHWHACKERS by B. J. Lanagan
An action-packed series by the creators of Longarm! The rousing adventures of the most brutal gang of cutthroats ever assembled—Quantrill's Raiders.

DIAMONDBACK by Guy Brewer
Dex Yancey is Diamondback, a Southern gentleman turned con man when his brother cheats him out of the family fortune. Ladies love him. Gamblers hate him. But nobody pulls one over on Dex . . .

WILDGUN by Jack Hanson
The blazing adventures of mountain man Will Barlow—from the creators of Longarm!

TEXAS TRACKER by Tom Calhoun
Meet J. T. Law: the most relentless—and dangerous—manhunter in all Texas. Where sheriffs and posses fail, he's the best man to bring in the most vicious outlaws—for a price.

JAKE LOGAN

SLOCUM
AND THE
BOUNTY JUMPERS

JOVE BOOKS, NEW YORK

SLOCUM AND THE BOUNTY JUMPERS

A Jove Book / published by arrangement with
the author

PRINTING HISTORY
Jove edition / May 2003

Copyright © 2003 by Penguin Putnam Inc.

For information address: The Berkley Publishing Group,
a division of Penguin Putnam Inc.,
375 Hudson Street, New York, New York 10014.

ISBN: 0-515-13531-3

A JOVE BOOK®
Jove Books are published by The Berkley Publishing Group,
a division of Penguin Putnam Inc.,
375 Hudson Street, New York, New York 10014.
JOVE and the "J" design
are trademarks belonging to Penguin Putnam Inc.

PRINTED IN THE UNITED STATES OF AMERICA

10 9 8 7 6 5 4 3 2 1

1

Another slug whizzed past Slocum's head. It spattered into the granite cliff face behind him before he had a chance to duck, and sent a rain of jagged shrapnel rock cting every which way.

Slocum hunkered down, however belatedly, if only because he had to reload. He hollered to Sam Biggle, his partner in this mess, "I thought these Conrad boys were bad shots. Ain't that what you been tellin' me, Sam?"

Sam, who was about fifteen feet away and hunched down behind the next big rock over, shouted back, "Goddamn it, Slocum, are you always so hoop-doodlin' facetious?"

Slocum leveled his rifle over the boulder again and took aim at a little patch of color—decidedly the wrong color for the Nevada desert.

"Yup," he said, and fired.

This time, there was a gratifying yelp after the shot, and that little patch of color suddenly got a lot bigger. It revealed itself to be a bright green-and-blue-checkered shirt, and it was on the prone body of Zeb Conrad, one of the boys they'd been hired to come out here after and whom they'd been tracking for the past four days.

"Believe you got one of 'em, there, ol' Long-Tall," called Sam.

"You get the other three," Slocum yelled back. He wiped the sweat from his brow and stared down the rifle again.

"Give me time, pardner, give me time."

Slocum pulled the trigger again, but missed. He cursed silently, but before the words had left his mouth, another of the Conrad boys suddenly stood straight up, grabbed at his chest, and fell over backward.

"Nice shot!" Slocum exclaimed. Sam was good with a gun, he'd sure give him that. Sam was good at a lot of things, and all-around good company too. You got to know a man when you spent four days in the saddle alongside him.

"Thank ye kindly," Sam said. "Just tryin' to hold up my end of the bargain."

The shots coming at them unexpectedly turned into a barrage that sang off rock, sent granite chips zinging like stinging shrapnel, and forced them both down low.

Slocum couldn't see Sam, but he could sure hear him when he shouted, "Believe they're tryin' to hold up their end too. Hoop-de-doodle-damn! Ain't them boys gonna run out of ammo any time soon?"

Just then they did, for the fire ended as suddenly as it had begun. Slocum quickly popped up and leveled his rifle while the last two Conrad boys reloaded. His eye caught a place where the brush was bent the wrong way, like somebody was back in there leaning on it, and he aimed low and just to the right of it.

He pulled the trigger.

Dread Conrad, the youngest and undoubtedly the meanest of the quartet, staggered from the bushes on his knees, a bright red stain spreading on his chest. He fell forward into the scrub onto his ugly, bucktoothed face. He didn't move again.

"Hot damn, Slocum!" Sam crowed from behind the next rock.

For the moment, Slocum ignored him. "Arvil?" he called. "Arvil Conrad! Dread and Corbett and Zeb are gone. You're all alone down there, Arvil. Why don't you give up and make it easy on everybody?"

Truth to tell, he didn't feel any too kindly, that last flurry of slugs having sent several granite chips zinging like fire into the back of his neck. He reached back and plucked the largest one out. His hand came away dripping with blood.

But he figured that you had to give people a chance, even low-down, murdering, worthless scum like the Conrad brothers. He'd tried talking to them before the fireworks commenced, to no avail.

"This is your last chance, Arvil!" he shouted again. "You're beginnin' to piss me off."

Arvil opened fire.

Aw, hell, Slocum thought, and popped up again, rifle at the ready.

But Sam was faster. Just as Slocum's head cleared the top of the rock, Sam fired. Arvil's body fell backward, out into the clear. It twitched once, and then went still.

"Hoop-de-doodle!" said Sam, standing lazily. "I do believe we're each two for two there, Slocum."

Sam was a long drink of water, just as tall as Slocum.

Blond and shaggy-headed, with a spade beard and tidy mustache, he was built like a scarecrow, all knees and elbows and angles. But unlike Slocum, who had a darker, more rugged charm—and the scars to go with it—Sam had the kind of blue-eyed, handsome face that the girls just loved. All kind of sweet and boyish, without the baby fat.

Of course, it helped that he was only twenty-four and therefore fifteen years younger than Slocum.

Sam made Slocum feel like an old man sometimes. Right now, for instance. His stance was as artless and relaxed as a sunning cougar, and a grin was on his face, as if he was out on a goddamn church picnic instead of a manhunt.

Slocum, on the other hand, was having to pull himself to his feet with handfuls of rock, and those grunts he was making didn't have a thing to do with pie or potato salad.

Not for the first time, Slocum said, "I'm gettin' too damn old for this."

"Don't be so hard on yourself there, Long-Tall," Sam said merrily, and gave him a hand up. "You got two of them bastards with just the one slug each."

"So did you," Slocum said, a bit crankily, and backed up a few feet, so that the rocks still shielded him from anybody down there who might not be all the way dead yet.

"Well," drawled Sam, "I figure you done it with a handicap, bein' as you're so elderly and all. Is that blood on your neck?"

"Damn rock splinters," said Slocum, and swiped at the wounds with his bandanna. "And shut up with that 'old' business." He tucked his bandanna away. "You'd best watch yourself, Sam, and we'd best get down there. I don't trust those buzzards not to play possum."

"Oh, they're dead, all right," said Sam, completely self-assured.

Just then, another shot sounded and took him in the shoulder.

He fell back, cursing, and without thinking, Slocum stepped forward, raised his rifle, and fired.

This time, Arvil Conrad went down for good.

Slocum went to the kid, who was grimacing and holding his arm.

"Damn and blast it!" Sam said through gritted teeth. "Reckon that makes you three for three there, Long-Tall."

"Reckon it does," Slocum muttered as he knelt down.

"You're gonna ruin my reputation," Sam said as Slocum quickly ripped away the kid's sleeve and took a look.

Sam wasn't hurt seriously. "Just hit the meat," Slocum said, and sat back on his heels. "You're sure one lucky whelp."

"Don't feel too lucky," Sam said, eyeing his arm. The wound was just below the joint of his shoulder, in the flesh of his upper arm. The slug had barely touched him, just left a nicely bleeding channel in the flesh, but Slocum knew it had to hurt like hell.

Well, a lesson was a lesson. He'd bet that Sam wouldn't be so careless next time.

"Bet you feel kinda dumb too," said Slocum, grinning. "Standin' up like that." He shook his head and helped Sam up. "They ain't dead all the way until they're underground. Remember that."

Sam got to his feet again, and shook Slocum off.

Slocum said, "You've still got a lot to learn, kid. Come on now. We'd best get that arm seen to."

"Aw, rub it in, why don't you?" Sam grumbled good-naturedly.

"The kid part or the learnin' part?"

"Both, goddamn it."

It fell to Slocum to do all the lifting and grunting. After he bandaged Sam's arm—and Sam saw to Slocum's neck—a grunting Slocum hoisted all four corpses atop their horses and tied them down. Fortunately, the place they were headed back to was a lot closer when you rode it as the crow flies, rather than when you were chasing four nasty, backtracking, gerrymandering, corkscrewing boys like the Conrads.

Slocum figured that he and Sam would get back up to Quicksand, Nevada, in about two days, maybe even a day and a half, which was a whole helluva lot quicker than it had taken them to get here. And the Conrads would just be starting to get rank about the time that they dropped them off and collected the fee.

That was fine with him. Let the city worry about putting them underground.

They rode on into the afternoon, Sam playing his harmonica sweet and low, and Slocum thinking about that money. He didn't usually go in for bounty kills, but the Conrads had done an old friend of his awful bad. That was Jeb Masterson, up in Quicksand. They'd killed his grown son, Matt, and Matt's wife, Clarissa, for nothing more than sport. At least, that's the way the story had unfolded.

Since the Conrads were already wanted dead or alive,

it didn't take Slocum more than a half second to say yes when Jeb's wire came. Course, he didn't know that he'd have to take on Matt's best friend, Sam, in the bargain.

But Sam had turned out to be pretty damn good company, and pretty trail-wise for somebody who was still so green around the edges. To tell the truth, Slocum would be sort of sorry to drop him off in Quicksand, along with the late Conrad brothers. The Conrad brothers, he'd be glad to leave off.

Jeb Masterson had offered Slocum two thousand dollars to bring them in, either way, and over and above the bounty. Slocum had found out that he'd offered the same to Sam. And that the both of them had turned him down flat. They'd split the government bounty, pure and simple—and eight thousand was a lot to split. No reason that Jeb should have to pay. He'd already paid enough, losing his son and daughter-in-law.

Sam must have been thinking about the same thing, because his harmonica music had taken a doleful turn. He finished up a particularly sorrowful rendition of "Streets of Laredo," then tapped the harmonica on the heel of his hand.

"Believe I'll hold off for a while, Slocum," he said, and tucked it into a vest pocket.

"My thinking exactly," Slocum replied. "Things are gettin' a little too much like a funeral around here."

Although considering the fact that they were leading four horses packed with four very dead bodies, the music couldn't have been more apropos.

Neither of them commented on this, however.

"You gonna stay on in Quicksand?" Slocum asked, expecting the answer to be yes.

"Hell, no," Sam said. "I only come back because of Matt and Clarissa. 'Cause they was murdered, I mean." He mopped at the back of his sunburnt neck with a bandanna. "No, I'll be movin' on. Goin' south, down to Arizona."

"What's there?"

Sam shrugged. "Stuff I ain't seen yet."

It was as good an answer as any.

Slocum, who was at loose ends as well, thought about this for a while. He figured he might as well head south too. After all, it was coming on fall. Arizona was a pretty decent place to hole up for the winter, so long as a body stayed out of the damned mountains.

"Mind if I ride along?" Slocum asked.

Sam was silent for a minute. And then he said, "I s'pose not."

"Don't go gettin' all overjoyed about it," Slocum said a little testily, although Sam's attitude didn't have him mad so much as curious. He hiked an eyebrow. "I can wander my way south all by my lonesome."

"No," Sam said, a lot faster this time. "I reckon I'd be pleased to have you along for the ride, Long-Tall. Won't have to do so much pathfindin' that way. And you're passable company."

Slocum shook his head. "Sam," he said, "you are one curious critter."

2

Sam and Slocum made it back up to Quicksand in a little over a day and a half, and rode into town just as the sun was setting.

It was none too soon either. The Conrad boys' bodies were beginning to bloat up and smell, well, pretty damn rank. It would only get worse, and so Slocum was happy to tie their horses to the hitching rail outside the sheriff's office and get away from the stench.

"There's your voucher," Sheriff Akins said, pushing a paper toward Sam from the other side of his desk. He was a shortish, portly man with most of his hair, and he seemed glad to have washed his hands of the matter.

Akins had been reluctant to offer more than a token posse at the time of the killings, and had done that much grudgingly, according to Jeb Masterson. The posse had spent exactly one day on the Conrads' trail, then ridden home empty-handed. And relieved. The Conrads were a bad bunch.

"Voucher?" asked Sam, staring at the paper in the light

9

of a lantern the sheriff had just lit. "I'd druther have my money, Sheriff Akins."

"I don't just keep eight thousand in my goddamn stove, Sam," the sheriff answered testily. "Think about it. Hell, you probably couldn't wring that much cash money out of the whole population if you squoze 'em."

"Well, where the hell do we have to go to collect?" Sam insisted.

"Carson City's the closest, I reckon," said Slocum. He was across the little office in the shadows, leaning against the wall with his arms crossed over his chest.

Akins jumped at the sound of his voice. "Hell, I near 'bout forgot you was there, Slocum," he said, rubbing at the back of his neck. "And yeah, I reckon they could take care of that"—he pointed to the voucher—"over to Carson City. It's a lot of money, y'know, eight thousand."

"You said that already," Sam growled.

"Well, it is!" snapped Akins.

Slocum stepped forward. "C'mon, Sam," he said. "Let's get the horses settled. I got my mind set on a bath and a steak and some female company, not necessarily in that order."

"Easy for you to say," Sam grumbled, staring dejectedly at the paper again. "You probably got more than a dollar-twenty to your name. And you ain't been shot up. Seems to me a man should get some cash money for bein' shot up."

"Don't worry, kid," said Slocum. He put his hand on Sam's shoulder and guided him to the door. "I'll stand you."

Just as Slocum opened the door, the sheriff piped up. "When you boys get down to the livery, you wanna send

Morris up here? Tell him I've got some bodies for him. And if you're wantin' Doc Stettler for that arm, Sam, his office is still over the saloon."

Slocum was riding a tall Appy gelding, dark bay and blanketed over his butt with a pure-white splash that was broken by exactly six big, fist-sized bay splotches. The gelding was young, only three and a half, and Slocum figured that by the time he was ten or twelve, his pattern would go all the way to leopard.

Slocum called the gelding Swampy. It wasn't the prettiest name, but he'd found him when he was just a weanling, all alone and sucked down in the mire and about ready to go under. Slocum had tossed a rope over the colt and hauled him out, christened him Swampy, and then left him with Joe Forbes, one of the best horsemen he knew.

Back then, when he left Swampy with Joe, the only things that had given a hint of Swampy's present coloration were his striped hooves, that ring of "human" white around his eyes, and a palm-sized spot of white on his rump. Now he was a flashy fifteen hands, neatly put together, and just coming into his own.

Slocum had just gotten around to retrieving Swampy a couple of months ago. He'd been pleased with what he found, despite the fact that Joe had seen fit to geld him.

"Dang horse was pure-D lunatic, Slocum!" Joe had said. "It was either cut him or shoot him."

Joe had done a good job on the gelding. Swampy was a good bit better than green-broke, already exhibiting a talent for reining. He stood still to shoot off, didn't spook at jackrabbits and the like, and could pick his way up and down steep shale or crumbling granite hills like a mountain goat.

Slocum figured that Swampy was going to make a damn fine mount.

Sam, on the other hand, seemed to be an Indian paint man. The mare on which he was mounted was bright chestnut and white, blue-eyed, and rangy. She was sure loud-colored, but it was belied by a calm disposition that Slocum hadn't expected when he first saw her. Sam called her Tess.

They rode up to the stable. The sign read,

> MORRIS P. FORD
> HORSES KEPT
> FURNITURE & UNDERTAKING
> GOD BLESS

"Reckon 'ol Morris is gonna save our horses from hellfire?" Slocum asked as he swung down off Swampy.

Sam didn't answer. "Morris?" he hollered. "Hey, Morris!"

"What, dag nab it?" came the reply, and Slocum looked inside the barn, then up, to see a bald head hanging upside down from the loft. The crisp blue eyes suddenly winged out in wrinkles. "Sam? Little Sammy Biggle? My Lordie, you has grown into a full-sized man and then some!"

The head pulled back up and disappeared, and a second later, Morris—all of him this time, five-foot-five and in the flesh—came down the loft ladder two rungs at a time.

He threw his arms around a grinning Sam, who had dismounted, and gave him a big hug. Then he stood back and held the kid out at arm's length.

"My goodness!" he said. "My goodness sakes! I heard

you was in town a few days back. Heard that you went out after them vile vermin what killed poor Matt and Clarissa."

"You heard right, Morris," Sam said. "The bodies are outside Akins's office. He said you can come get 'em any time."

Morris took a step back and slapped a hand over his heart. "You done it?" he asked incredulously. "You already got the Conrads? All four of 'em? And they's dead? Saints alive!"

"Well, I got one anyway," Sam said quickly, and flushed just a hair. "This here's Slocum, Morris," he added quickly. "I reckon he accounted for three of 'em."

"More like two and a half," Slocum said, and took Morris's swiftly offered hand. "You would've been right proud of Sam here."

The old man tipped his head. "Slocum? Did he say your name was Slocum?"

Slocum nodded.

"My stars," said Morris slowly, his eyes big as saucers. "There can't be that many fellas named Slocum who ride an Appaloosa and go round killin' the murderous likes of the Conrads. Why, I got me a bona fide legend standin' right smack in my barn!"

Slocum opened his mouth to argue, but Morris had turned away. "And a legend in the making!" he said to Sam. "Judas-over-the-cliff! It's a red-letter day, all right!"

3

Slocum opted for the bath first

The bathhouse was small but cozy, with dark, unfinished wooden walls, long benches for getting dressed or undressed, a curtained shitter in the back, and a couple of Chinese boys to fetch and carry the hot water. Good Kentucky bourbon was available, as well as bubbles for your bath, cigars or cigarettes or good pipe tobacco, and a two-chair barbershop out front. If a fellow had the time, the wherewithal, and the inclination, there was opium in a side room.

Slocum wasn't interested in the opium, though.

He was the only customer in the bathhouse portion of the establishment, and he'd been there awhile, soaking in a deep, wide tub of warm, soapy water, a cigar clenched between his white teeth, his eyes peacefully half-lidded.

Then Sam Biggle came in, signaled to the Chinese kids to bring the buckets, stripped off, and hopped into the next tub with a splash.

"Hoop-de-doodle!" said Sam as he sank down in the steaming water. One of the Chinese boys dumped another pail in. "I'll be danged if that don't feel mighty good!"

Slocum roused enough to flick the suds off his hand. He reached over to the stool between the tubs and poured himself another shot from the bottle sitting there. Thoughtfully, he twirled it in his fingers. "What'd the doc say about your arm?" he asked around the cigar.

Sam picked up a bar of soap and began scrubbing at his elbow. "Same thing you said. He reckoned I'll live. Said I ain't got an infection, and that if I dump some high-proof joy juice on it every night till it's healed, I'll live to be a hundred and fifty-five. Give or take."

Slocum knocked back his whiskey, then sucked in air through his teeth. It was mighty fine bourbon, a hundred and one proof. "That's comfortin'," he said. "Although I've got to tell you, I think that doc of yours is a tad optimistic." He set the shot glass back on the stool with a little thump.

"That's what I said." Sam began to work at the other arm. "I figure a hundred and twenty tops. When we goin' out to tell Jeb and Martha?"

"First thing in the morning, I reckon."

It would give Slocum a great deal of pleasure to tell Jeb and his wife that their boy's death had been avenged. Not as much pleasure as bringing Matt and Clarissa Masterson back to life, of course, but he had done everything humanly possible aside from that. He hoped it would help to ease their hearts.

Sam, concentrating on soaping his toes, nodded. "So what's next? Women or dinner?"

"I must be gettin' old," Slocum said around his cigar. "Dinner."

The Chinese boy, waiting patiently in the corner beside the stove, snickered.

"You sure are if you're thinkin' that way," Sam said just a little too goddamned happily. "But I reckon I could use me a nice steak before I start workin' up a sweat."

Slocum glared at him. "Nice of you."

Grinning, Sam worked the soap up his calf. "I thought it was."

Quicksand only claimed a little over seven hundred souls in residence, but it was possessed of a pretty damn fine whorehouse. It was called Kitty's Cat's Moow, and was run by one Kitty Muldoon, who said she was from Fresno, out in California. Kitty was a youngish thirty who didn't show a whit of gray in her auburn hair. Slocum suspected she used henna, but he only thought of it afterward, and even then, it was hardly worth commenting on.

Sam picked out a pretty little blonde by the name of Honeysuckle Rose, and escorted her upstairs with his hat in his hand, a shit-eating grin on his face, and a big bulge in the front of his britches.

Slocum followed with Kitty.

The upstairs reminded him of the inside of the bath-house. With rough hewn timbers and rougher floors, the building had been thrown up in a hurry and wasn't meant to last.

Course, that was the way it was in most of these mining towns. Folks knew the ore deposits would wear out and be mined out, and then they'd move on. No use in building houses to stand through the ages. Most everything about Quicksand had a real temporary feel to it.

Even the whores.

Kitty'd had hungry eyes for him the moment he walked in the place, and Slocum was thinking that he'd prefer a more experienced woman anyway. She was that, by the looks of it. At least, she sure didn't stand on ceremony. She was out of her corset and knickers before Slocum could say, "Howdy," and had him out of his britches before he could say, "Thanks!"

She was freckled all over, and had enormous, round, full breasts with dark pink nipples. Her hips were full, and she had a cute little potbelly that hung partway over the triangle of red fur at the juncture of her legs.

He didn't get much chance to enjoy looking, though, because she had him down on the straw mattress in slap time.

Of course, it wasn't like he tried to fight her off or anything.

"What'd you say your name was?" Kitty asked just before she licked him straight across his chest.

"Slocum," he said, and planted both hands on her fanny. It was a big fat one, and he liked it. More to hang on to that way.

She paused mid-lick, and looked him right in the eye. "Slocum? *The* Slocum? You and your friend the ones what brought in the Conrad boys?"

Slocum cocked a brow. "Depends."

"On what?"

"On whether the Conrads was friends of yours or not."

She cocked a brow and slid a hand down to grab hold of him where it mattered. "Weren't no friends of mine," she whispered as she gently ran her thumb over the bulbous head. "That damned old Arvil owed me a buck-fifty, and his brother Dread was meaner'n a bucket full a goaded badgers. He beat up my Patsy gal a month ago. Give her a black eye and everything. Friends of mine? I should say not!"

"Well, then, honey, I'm right sorry about your loss," Slocum said with a very aroused grin. Kitty was working miracles down there on his John Henry, and without even concentrating on it!

He curled one hand under her butt and between her legs, and slid a couple of fingers inside her. She was hot and she was sure wet. "And yeah, the kid and I brought 'em in."

Slit-eyed, she ground her hips against his fingers "Baby, this one's on the house."

The next morning, a very relaxed Slocum set out for Jeb Masterson's place, Sam Biggle at his side. Sam was in an awfully good mood too, which he expressed by talking nonstop.

Slocum let him get away with it, though. He was still flying higher than an eagle on last night and the amazing Kitty Muldoon.

God bless chubby women. Oh, the young ones and the trim and the sleek ones were fine and dandy. He admired them too. But if and when he ever settled down, he was going to find him a nice, fat, round-hipped, big-butted woman to share his life and his bed. No bones to poke him, and no sharp edges.

Hell, he had enough sharp edges for three people all by himself.

No, just soft, womanly curves, big breasts, and all that lush flesh to keep him warm on cold nights. And they were grateful too, goddamn it. Plus, he secretly thought that they were softer on the inside, in their hearts, bless 'em.

Sam had been carrying on for half the morning, and Slocum had listened to exactly none of it, being caught up in his own thoughts about round-hipped women and all. So when they stopped at about ten to rest the horses and Sam all of a sudden grabbed him by the arm and turned him around, it came as something of a surprise.

"Well? What do you think, ol' Long-Tall?" he asked.

And when Slocum just stared at him, he added, "You ain't heard a word I've said, have you?"

Slocum shrugged. "Can't rightly say that I have, Sam." He loosened Swampy's girth, then pulled down his water bag.

Sam raised his eyes heavenward. "Cripes!" he shouted. "You listenin' now?"

"Reckon so." Slocum watered his horse.

"For the last five miles I been talkin' about this damn reward voucher," Sam said. He loosened Tess's girth too, and poured water into a canvas feed bag. He held it out, and the paint mare dipped her nose inside eagerly.

"And?" Slocum asked. He figured they'd be out to Jeb's place by about noon. He hoped that Martha would have a big mess of her good beef stew simmering on the stove. Maybe she'd bake up some of those special fried biscuits of hers, with fresh butter and mesquite honey. Nothing like them in the whole world!

Just thinking about it had his mouth watering.

Damn, he *was* getting old!

"And what do you think?"

"About what?" Slocum asked a bit testily.

Sam snatched off his hat and threw it on the ground.

"Dad-blast it! Will you listen to me, consarn you? I just told you. You want I should tear it in half or what?"

"Tear what in half?"

"The consarned hoop-de-doodlin' voucher, goddamn it!" Sam shouted.

"Hold your water, Sam," Slocum said.

"Dang it, Slocum—"

Pointing, Slocum cut him off. "I mean, really hold it. You're drippin' on your boots."

Sam snatched at his water bag, which he'd let slip away from Tess's muzzle, and straightened it. The mare was grateful.

Sam was a little embarrassed, though, by the looks of it.

"Doggone it," he muttered, then loudly said, "You listenin' now?"

"Both ears," Slocum said. "Promise."

"All right. Seein' as how you've got the attention span of a gnat this mornin', I'll make it quick."

Slocum grinned. "Obliged."

"I was thinkin' that mayhap I ought'a rip this voucher—the one that's burnin' a hole in my pocket—into two pieces."

"Why?"

Sam rolled his eyes. "Well, because there's two of us, that's why. That way, if somethin' happens to me—I mean, if I should fall off a cliff or somethin'—you can still take half of it to Carson City."

Swampy had finished drinking, and Slocum shook the last drops from the feed bag and folded it up. "And what would that do for me?" he asked.

"Well, I mean, you could show it to 'em. They could

mayhap wire Sheriff Akins to verify that it was on the up and up."

Slocum shoved the feed bag back inside his saddlebag, them poked around in his pocket for his fixings bag. "You ain't thought about this too much, have you, Sam?"

Sam's head jerked up. "Hell, I thought about it all last night." And then he colored. "Well, after I got done at Kitty's place, I mean."

Slocum's mouth quirked up into a smile. As he rolled up his smoke, he said, "Tell you what, Sam. Why don't you just hold on to that paper? That way, if something was to happen to me, you'd get your money just fine."

He paused to roll up his quirlie, and he gave it a final lick. "And if something was to happen to you, you can bet your butt that I'd turn over heaven and earth to get that paper back."

Sam's face twisted. "That makes me feel some better. I think. But still, it's vexin' me. Wouldn't you rather—"

"Sam?" Slocum cut in. "Just put a lid on it."

Now eight thousand dollars was a whole lot of money. Slocum supposed that it was more than a lot of men would see in their whole lifetimes. Even half of it, four thousand, was a powerful lot.

He planned on divvying it up even, right down the middle, although he hadn't said as much to Sam. And even though he himself had shot three of the Conrad boys.

After all, he figured to just spend it on good champagne and good cigars and bad women. And four thousand could buy a whole helluva lot of any of those things.

To Sam, four thousand probably represented his future: a ranch of his own, maybe even a little business. After all, he was young. As he kept pointing out.

Sam sagged a little and gave his head a doleful shake. "All right, Slocum. But I think you got bats in your belfry."

Slocum shook out his match and took a draw on his smoke. "That's me," he said without any expression whatsoever. "Batty. Just a regular devil-may-care sonofabitch."

He led Swampy into the deep purple shade of several paloverde trees, ground-tied him, then slumped down, his back against a boulder.

"I don't know about you, Sam," he allowed, "but I'd sure like to sit for a spell on somethin' that ain't movin'."

He pulled his hat down over his eyes, and let his head loll back.

He heard Sam grumble, "Well, turds!" and then heard the sound of Sam's horse's hooves as he led it too into the deeper shade.

"Sometimes, Slocum," Sam muttered, "I just can't figure you for beans."

4

"Hurry up, Mariah!" Joe snapped.

Mariah Clemm fanned the old buckskin's rump again, although it didn't do much good, then grabbed at her bonnet. It was about to fly straight off her head.

Joe reached over and cut the aging buckskin across the rump with his quirt, and it finally bounded into a lope. Mariah nearly lost her seat, and clung to the saddlehorn like a tick to a dog's back.

Drat Joe anyway! Why did she have to do this?

Joe laughed. At her, she supposed. He could be so mean! It wasn't her fault that she couldn't ride very well. It wasn't her fault that she was out here in the first place. She should have been back in Ohio, should have taught school, married and had kids, and worked a little patch of land alongside her husband. Maybe sung in the church choir of a Sunday. She had no business here, not in Nevada, for God's sake!

And she certainly had no business being totally, unequivocally, completely single at twenty-eight.

An old maid, she thought as she clung to the cantering

gelding. *I'm an old maid. Threw away my future on Billy Bob Carlisle, that no-good sonofabitch, and look at me now, twenty-eight and a half, long ago spoiled goods, and riding an aging bronc through the desert. And for what? Another one of Joe Harper's stupid schemes, that's what.*

She was going to leave him.

Of course, she'd been going to leave him for something like five years.

All she needed was a chunk of cash, enough to give her a good stake so that she could go back home and buy some land or a little milliner's shop or something. She supposed she wouldn't mind being single for the rest of her life if only she could hold her head up.

But every time it looked like she had a chance, every time it looked like maybe she could break away, get free, something happened right at the very last minute. Either Joe screwed it up or she did.

That badger game they'd been running in Bisbee? That one went bad all of a damn sudden, with the loveliest mark all fat and juicy and set up proper, and then that big, fat sheriff coming in through the window with his guns drawn. She and Joe had left town so fast that she'd even left behind her mother's silver hairbrush.

And then up in Idaho Springs they'd been inches away from a big windfall, with Cyrus T. Peckinpah about to hand over the deed to a hundred thousand acres of virgin timberland.

Well, that one had been her fault, she guessed. But how the hell was she supposed to know that Cyrus was allergic to strawberries? He'd collapsed, head-first, into his fruit surprise seconds before signing the papers. Actually, this wouldn't have been so bad, but the mayor was with them at the dinner party to witness the signing, and thus Joe couldn't even try to forge Cyrus's name.

Oh, Joe would never let her hear the last of that one.

Which was one reason that the old buckskin was cantering on the heels of Patsy's bay.

Patsy was a silly, snippy little thing. Only eighteen years old. Prettier than all get-out, though, Mariah admitted reluctantly. And she could ride, damn her. She was up there sitting that horse like she'd been born on his back, while Mariah was back here, eating her dust, with Joe on his chestnut beside her, repeatedly slashing the old buckskin across his bony rump.

She'd like to give that stupid quirt to the buckskin and turn him loose on Joe, that's what she'd like to do.

She'd have whipped Joe herself if he hadn't promised her on a stack of Bibles that this was the big one. Eight thousand dollars, he'd said, and her cut would be two grand.

A girl could go a long way from Joe Harper, and a long way east of the Mississippi, on two thousand.

And so she ground her teeth, closed her eyes against the stinging grit, and tried not to think about the horse laboriously groaning beneath her.

Slocum and Sam rode into Jeb Masterson's ranch, the Lazy M, at just past noon. Martha shed a few tears and Jeb sniffed and turned away for a moment when Slocum told them that Matt and Clarissa had been avenged, and Slocum and Sam each got a big hug from Martha and a solemn handshake from Jeb.

And dinner, of course. Martha pulled out all the stops.

Afterward, while Jeb and Slocum and Sam sat out on

the porch, admiring the afternoon and smoking cigars, Jeb said, "I can't rightly thank you boys enough. I just wish you'd let me give you something."

Sam shook his head, and Slocum said, "We been all through this, Jeb. Government's payin' us a bounty, and that's plenty." He glowered, then added, "Truth to tell, I would'a gone out after those sonsabitches for no money at all."

"Same goes for me," said Sam. "Just the doin' of it was enough, Jeb. Just wish that we could'a brought ol' Matt and Clarissa back." His eyes grew a touch misty, and he turned away from them for a moment.

Jeb did much the same, which left Slocum staring at his cigar. After a moment, he said, "Well, what's done is done, hard as it may be to swallow. And Sam? We'd best be gettin' on."

Old Jeb Masterson cleared his throat. "So soon? Me and Martha figured you'd be putting up for the night."

"No, Slocum's right," Sam said. He gave a cursory rub to his eyes, then stood up. "We're headed for Carson City. Then we're thinkin' that mayhap we'll head down Arizona way. Soon as I make me another trip to your outhouse, that is," he added with a grin.

As he stepped down off the porch and started around the house, Jeb quietly said, "That's sure a mighty fine boy."

Slocum nodded. "Agreed. He did himself proud out there."

"You too, Slocum," Jeb said around his cigar, and then his eyes narrowed. "When you were out settling the horses, Sam told us as how you took down three of those murdering skunks. I wish you could have killed 'em all six times over."

"Know how you feel, Jeb," Slocum said quietly. "But killin' a man once is usually enough."

Jeb reached into his hip pocket, saying, "I know you won't take cash money, Slocum. But I'm hoping you won't turn down a gift."

He produced a silver flask, a fancy one with a big gold eagle fixed on the front, and handed it to Slocum.

It was heavy in Slocum's hand. It must have cost a pretty penny once upon a time. "I don't rightly know what to say, Jeb," Slocum allowed.

Jeb smiled. Just a little. "Then don't say a thing. I already filled it up with my best Kentucky bourbon, the stuff I keep for Christmas."

Slocum nodded and tucked the flask in his breast pocket. "Thanks, Jeb."

Jeb nodded. "I'd take Summit Pass if I was you. Best way to get through the mountains, if you've got your heart set on Carson City." He scratched his head. "Only way, come to think of it, unless you want to cut way down to the southeast. That's a long, hot ride, though."

Slocum nodded. He knew the trail, a long, winding pass through the hills that eventually led you within thirty miles of Carson City. He'd traveled it a few times before.

They sat there in silence for a few minutes, until Sam came striding around the side of the house.

"Say, that's sure a mighty fine outhouse you built yourself there, Jeb," he drawled, a big grin on his face. "Got a Sears catalog on the side shelf and everythin'!"

•   •   •

The buckskin was all in, poor thing, and Joe finally had to stop.

Mariah slid down off the horse gratefully, and leaned against his lathered flank for a moment, just to get steady on her legs again. The poor old nag was in sad shape, and she almost felt sorrier for him than for herself.

Joe had dismounted too, because suddenly he was at her side, pushing her away, and hurriedly stripping the saddle and bridle off the buckskin. The horse groaned softly.

"Get up behind Patsy," Joe said.

"Give him some water first," Mariah responded, partly out of mercy, and partly because getting up on a horse again was the last thing she wanted to do right now.

"Women," said Joe with a snort, and tossed her a water bag. She caught it, and staggered back under its weight.

"Hope you didn't mean that derogatory, Joe," said Patsy, who had also dismounted and was leading her mount around in small circles. "And you'd best keep that nag moving if you don't want him goin' all sickly on you."

Mariah looked up from her palm, from which the buckskin was lipping water. She glanced from Patsy to Joe, who was grudgingly walking his horse too, and then back at her old buckskin.

"Just a little," she whispered to the horse, "and then you've got to walk too. Not that I care or anything."

She poured out a bit more water—it was her fifth or sixth palmful—then tried to convince the animal to move.

She had no luck. Joe had quirted and lashed the horse into the ground, and it was plain that Joe planned to leave him behind to die. She picked up the worn bridle from the ground, where Joe had tossed it away, wrapped the reins around the horse's neck, and gave them a tug. The buckskin moved forward a few steps, then stopped, then sank down to his knees with a loud moaning sound.

Mariah dropped the bridle.

"He's done," Joe said. "Get up behind Patsy."

He was looking down at her from astride his tall mount. He wasn't the handsomest man, old Joe, but he did have what her mother used to call a commanding presence. Sort of a military bearing, she supposed.

He was blond, or had been. Now his close-cropped hair was shot through with silver. He was lean and had a pronounced nose, and the nicest blue eyes she had ever seen. They said, "Trust me, I'm your pal," even when he was about to lift your purse, screw your sister, or sell you a nonexistent bridge.

"Can't you do something to help him?" Mariah asked, pointing at the buckskin. He was all the way down on his side now, breathing heavily, his eyelids half closed.

"Sure," said Joe, and before she realized it, he'd drawn his gun and sent a bullet into the poor beast's skull.

"What'd you do that for?" she shouted, caught between alarm at the suddenness and surprise of it, and the fact that she hadn't meant for him to kill the animal.

Joe shrugged. "You said to." He slid his side arm back into its holster.

Patsy tittered.

"Shut up!" Mariah barked at her. "Just shut your mouth."

Joe reined his horse away from Mariah, giving her a clear path to Patsy. "Now, Mariah," he said.

And while she marched toward Patsy's horse, her hands

balled into fists, Joe added, "I'm leavin' you here. Patsy knows the rest of the way to the pass. Right, Patsy?"

"Right," said Patsy, making too much of her groan as she helped Mariah mount up behind her. It was probably her way of letting Joe know that Mariah had gotten too fat. Either that, or to reinforce that she was such a tiny, frail thing.

I'll show her how frail, Mariah thought as she settled, rather uncomfortably, behind the saddle. *I'll show her with a knuckle punch, the little bitch.*

"You both got the story?" Joe asked. Again. How stupid did he think they were?

"Yes, Joe," they said in unison.

"All right," he replied as he gathered his reins. "I won't be far off. And don't go killin' each other in the meantime."

"We're supposed to just get there and wait," said Patsy, and Mariah rolled her eyes.

"That's right," said Joe, and threw her a quick grin.

Unconsciously, Mariah pulled her head back. She didn't want to catch it, no way.

Joe saw her, though, and frowned. "Aw, just get goin'," he grumbled.

Patsy started the horse moving at a slow jog, and Mariah turned her head to watch Joe slowly disappear into the distance. "The rat bastard," she said.

"Why?" piped up Patsy. " 'Cause he shot that damn horse of yours? You knew we was only gonna take one of 'em into the pass with us. That was the plan all along."

"I know the plan, you little dolt," Mariah said. "I just thought he'd turn it loose or something, that's all."

Patsy shrugged her slender shoulders. "What's the dif-

ference? You're gonna be rich. Buy another horse. Buy a
whole string of horses for all I care. Me, I'm gonna buy
me the fanciest whorehouse west of Omaha. A real hum-
dinger!"

"I'll just bet," Mariah muttered. She spat out a strand
of Patsy's long, white-blond hair that had strayed into her
mouth. At least *she* had a hair color—dark, dark brown—
that didn't need to be helped along with peroxide and
lemon juice and bluing and God knows what else. Patsy's
hair was like straw.

"You're just jealous," Patsy said stiffly. "You're just fit
to be tied because I'm young and pretty and you're old
and washed up."

Mariah bit the inside of her cheek for a moment, until
the urge to haul off and push Patsy off the horse passed.
"I'm not jealous, you stupid strumpet," she finally said.
"I just want something different, that's all."

"I'll say!" Patsy blurted out with a little laugh. "You
wanna go back East and marry up with some farmer or
something! Well, you can give me the nightlife! Give me
smoky rooms and good Kentucky bourbon and hungry
men—and I don't mean for food—every damn time."

"You can have 'em, sister," Mariah muttered. "And
isn't there a more comfortable gait we can travel at? Another quarter mile of this and my fanny's gonna be
pounded beefsteak."

"Sure," said Patsy, just a little too happily, and urged
the gelding into a lope. Which knocked Mariah lopsided.

"Damn it!" Mariah shouted, and hung onto Patsy's
waist for dear life.

5

Slocum figured it would take him and Sam about two and a half, maybe three days to get down to Carson City. They had ridden out of Jeb Masterson's ranch that afternoon, bearing parcels of cold chicken and thick brown bread from Martha and weighed down by the solemn gratitude of Jeb.

"I'll be back by to see you one of these days," Sam had shouted over his shoulder. "You can count on it!"

Jeb and Martha had just kept waving until they disappeared from sight.

And now Slocum and Sam Biggle were working their way into the hills. It'd be about fifteen or twenty minutes before they'd come to the start of Summit Pass.

The pass wasn't showy or anything. In fact, you could ride a mile down into it before you realized you were in the pass at all. Sometimes, even then, greenhorns didn't recognize it for what it was. Slocum wasn't certain what had created it—maybe a long-ago earthquake or some primordial river, long gone—but it made a convenient cut through the mountains for nearly thirty-five miles. Another thirty after you came out the other end, you were in Carson City. Course, those last thirty were the easiest.

Summit Pass was both a blessing and a curse for those pilgrims coming north from Carson City or going south toward it. It made travel a helluva lot easier, but it was also a prime spot for bushwhackers and road bandits and holdup artists. Plenty of places to hide out in, to strike from fast and quick, and to scurry away through.

He hadn't mentioned this to Sam. The kid was already nervous enough about that damned voucher he carried. Slocum saw him touch his breast pocket every now and then, as if he was just making sure the stiff little hump of folded paper was still there.

Well, Slocum didn't figure they'd have a problem. They sure didn't look rich, that was for certain. They just looked like a couple of saddle bums. Which was what they were, he supposed. Nobody in their right mind would rob them.

They wouldn't even try, if they got a look at Slocum close up.

But still, he was going to be a little on the nervous side until they came out the other end.

Joe Harper had lollygagged around until he figured it was safe, and then he'd cut east, toward the Masterson place. Sure enough, he sighted them leaving about a half hour later.

He kept them locked in the binoculars' sights until they could no longer be seen, and then he mounted up and set off after them at a slow jog.

He was in no hurry.

He whistled softly under his breath, and smiled.

And now they were nearly to the mouth of the pass.

He loved the town of Quicksand. Well, he supposed he should say that he loved towns *like* Quicksand. Everybody was so nice and chatty.

He didn't suppose that Mr. Famous Slocum and that pup Sam Biggle had been in town twenty minutes before the entire populace knew their business, and that they intended to stop by the Masterson ranch on their way out of town.

And that they had a voucher for eight thousand burning a hole in their pockets.

Joe didn't know about anybody else, but that little snippet of news had surely made his day.

They'd take the pass, of course. Everybody did.

Now, at first he'd been thinking about robbing them in the pass and trying to cash in the voucher himself. But after a moment's consideration, that didn't wash. Slocum was some sort of famous *pistolero* or something. At least, he was well known. A few of the men in the bar where he'd heard the news had lifted their eyebrows at the mention of his name.

A few more had said, "Slocum, eh? No wonder them damn Conrad boys is dead."

Joe Harper's line of work didn't often cross with gunfighters, but he knew enough about them in general to know that he'd have to take them from ambush. He was a pretty fair shot, but only when he had time to aim.

Joe was no shootist, and he knew it.

Besides, the rumor was that the sheriff had made a trip down to the telegrapher's office shortly after accepting the Conrads' bodies. Joe figured that the telegram had gone right straight to the Carson City sheriff.

These lawmen! All of them, in each others' pockets. He shook his head ruefully and clicked his tongue. Typical.

Ah, well. He'd come to the conclusion that he'd best let them cash in their stupid voucher on their own. But he wasn't going to let them get away, not with all that money, no, sir! He'd need bait, and he had just the thing: Mariah Clemm and Patsy Himmel.

They were just the right ages too, he figured. Pasty would do for Sam Biggle, and Mariah for Slocum. They both knew their trade, although Mariah was better at it than Patsy. More practice, he supposed. But Patsy more than made up for it in eagerness.

Mariah, on the other hand, was on her way out of the business. Some gals just couldn't take it for too long, he supposed. Just as well. She was getting too old and too fat. He hadn't slept with her in over five years.

He liked to think that had been his idea, but in truth, Mariah had slammed the door in his face too many times. Highfalutin little wench.

Oh, well.

By now, he thought, the girls were somewhere up ahead in the pass, artfully draped over a couple of rocks and looking lost and hopeless and helpless, and waiting for the sound of those two bums' approaching hoofbeats.

He smiled again and let his horse plod on. He knew exactly where Slocum and Biggle were going. He had all the time in the world.

By the time Sam noticed that they were in a pass, with hills rising up on either side and the vegetation slowly changing from low desert scrub to chaparral, they were already in about a half a mile.

Or so said Slocum.

"Now, just how do you figure exactly where it started there, ol' Long-Tall?" he teased. "Didn't seem to me like there was a sign or anythin'."

Slocum snorted and reined that Appy of his around another bush.

"It also don't seem to me like there's much of a road," Sam went on. There was no road at all, in fact. Just a sort of brushy path where there were no trees or sizable vegetation.

"Nope," Slocum said. "No road."

"That's what I like about you, Slocum," Sam said amiably. "You're so damned talkative. Why, you can keep a conversation goin' all day long. Never a dull moment with you!"

Characteristically, Slocum grunted, but that was all.

He had surely got himself hitched up with a peculiar sort of fellow, Sam thought. He liked Slocum, though. He liked him fine.

Now, Sam could take care of himself. He'd been on his own for more years than he liked to count. He was fast with a handgun and pretty damn slick with a rifle, even if he had sort of missed his target back there on that Conrad feller.

Well, his sights must be a smidgen off, that's what it was. And he'd knocked the bastard down, hadn't he?

He sniffed.

Slocum didn't seem to notice.

Good old Slocum. Just having him around made Sam feel sort of . . . safe. Safer, he should have said. There was something about the man that made you feel like he was invulnerable, and like anything you tried in tandem with him would go through just fine.

Maybe it was all those scars. Sam had seen just a few of them on his arms and throat, and by the looks of it, the rest of him must be as crisscrossed and puckered and marked up with scar tissue as the parts Sam could see.

Yessir, Slocum was a man who'd seen a lot of trail. And some of it face-first, by the looks of him.

For the first time in years, Sam was actually relaxed. For once, he didn't have to be the one to watch for bad men or Indians or bad women. Although he still watched, make no mistake about that. Old habits died hard. But he always had the feeling that Slocum, bless his beat-up heart, was going to see any threat before he did.

It was actually a very comforting thing, riding with a legend.

It was also a comforting thing, thinking about that money just waiting for them. Two thousand dollars! That'd be his cut, he figured. After all, he'd only take one of the Conrads out. But two thousand was a lot of money.

He was thinking a little about a certain valley he'd been through, a valley in northern Arizona. Tall grass, good grazing land, a place where a man might sink down some roots and get off whatever trail he was on. Settle down. Well, he hadn't quite figured that out.

Maybe it was time to try.

As much as he admired Slocum, he didn't want to end up like him. He didn't have the makings for it, not down in his heart. And he knew damn well that if he kept on going like he was, that was exactly how he'd end up: looking forty in the face, constantly on the move, going from odd job to odd job (which usually entailed gun work), and with no woman to call his own.

If he was lucky enough to live that long.

No, the life was fine for some, but Sam was beginning to have second thoughts. That valley had started to pop into his dreams every now and then, and he'd even built an imaginary house on it. Just a little cabin with a front room and kitchen and a bedroom, nothing fancy.

And there was a woman in the bedroom, a woman whose face was unknown to him as yet. But she was there, all right, and she was his. Sometimes, in his dreams, he could hear her humming or singing softly, back in the darkness of that imaginary bedroom in that imaginary ranch house.

"Aw, you're loco," he muttered.

Slocum looked over and cocked a brow.

"Don't mind me," Sam said, a little embarrassed.

"Never do," said Slocum. And then, quite suddenly, he reined in his Appy.

Sam reined in his paint too. "What?"

Slocum was already reaching for his spyglass. "Don't know yet," he said.

He put the glass to his eye and stared though it while Sam waited impatiently. If Slocum had sighted a passel of bandits up there, Sam would just as soon turn right around and go the long way to Carson City, and he planned on telling Slocum that flat out. He wasn't about to take a chance on losing two thousand dollars—at least the potential of two thousand dollars—to a bunch of mossy-toothed bushwhackers.

But then again, he thought, there might only be just

three or four of them. And they might be worth some money.

He rolled his eyes. *Sam Biggle,* he scolded himself, *you are just gettin' too money-hungry for words! And besides, it's probably only a deer up ahead. Maybe a cougar, considering the way he's staring though that thing.*

"I'll be damned," Slocum said, and folded the spyglass. "I'll just be damned."

"What is it you see up there?" asked Sam testily, sitting forward in his saddle. "How long you gonna keep me in suspense?"

"Women," replied Slocum. "Looks like a couple of women with horse trouble."

6

"Here they come," whispered Patsy. She was perched on a big boulder right out in the clear, and she made a show of baring one bent knee and studying it.

Mariah snorted softly. "You know, Patsy," she said in weary disgust, "the more I think about it, the more I believe a whorehouse is just the sort of place you ought'a buy."

Patsy's eyes narrowed. "What's that supposed to mean?"

"Just what it sounded like," Mariah said with a sigh. She held up a hand to shade her eyes. "I see them now too. Just barely. All right, they've had a good gander. Come on, let's get moving."

Mariah ran to grab the horse, and began to head back into the thicker brush at the edge of the trees. But she stopped halfway there.

"Are you coming or what?" she hissed at Patsy. "Stop preening and move it!"

Patsy didn't budge. "What're you going over there for?" she hissed back.

"Come on! They might be killers or something!"

"But we know they aren't!" Patsy stage-whispered with a roll of her eyes.

Mariah ground her teeth. "But they don't know that we know that, you idiot!"

"Oh," said Patsy, the light suddenly dawning. "Okay," she said, and scrambled off the rock somewhat belatedly.

"Hold up there, ladies! We don't mean you no harm," Sam called.

The women were almost to the trees, leading a tired bay gelding behind them. With his spyglass, Slocum had checked again just to make certain the women were truly alone. That was about halfway after he'd first sighted them. They looked to be on the up and up, but he still had a nervous feeling. It would be just his luck if a whole passel of bandits rode down out of the trees right about now.

But there were no bandits, and the women stopped and turned toward Longarm and Sam, albeit suspiciously. There was a young blonde, kind of frizzy-haired and pretty, and a brunette, rounded nice in the hips and bosom, just like he liked them.

Slocum felt a stirring and a stiffening in his britches, but willed it away.

He called, "Afternoon, ladies," and tipped his hat. "You in a speck of trouble?"

The brunette called right back, "What makes you think that?"

Slocum grinned just a little. He liked a gal with spunk. Of course, they'd probably turn out to be two missionaries who'd lost their load of Bibles or been robbed of a whole wagon load of crucifixes. Bible-thumpers weren't usually interested in his favorite sport, indoor or otherwise.

"Well, you're out here, ain't you?" Slocum called, and pushed the hat back on his forehead. "There's only one horse between you, and by the looks of his track he picked up a stone a good piece back. He's limpin', in case you hadn't noticed."

The brunette, who had charge of the horse, scowled at him, then led the horse forward a few feet. He limped, all right. She shook her head.

Sam called, "We'd be pleased to escort you ladies down to Carson City, if that's where you're headed. We're goin' that way ourselves, and we'd be glad for the company."

"Speak for yourself," Slocum grumbled. The brown-haired gal was pretty, all right, and padded in all the right places, but he'd reminded himself that there was no "for sale" sign anywhere on her. Plus she was wearing a high-necked dress—not the usual garb for a woman who was interested—and a prim little bonnet. And they were both brown, just a little lighter than the color of her hair.

A missionary, for certain.

"Be obliged!" called the blond one, just like that, and started toward them.

Sam broke out in a great big grin, but it fell when the brunette grabbed her companion's arm and shouted, "How do we know you aren't robbers or highwaymen? I can tell you right now, we've got nothing for you to steal."

The blonde shook her arm free and rubbed it petulantly. "They look fine to me, Mariah," she said. "Just fine."

Right about then, Slocum noticed that the blonde was attired a little more casually than the brunette. Mariah, was it? And he also noticed that Sam was making calf eyes at the blonde. Jesus, save him from youngsters!

"Oh, we're honest and upstandin', ma'am," Sam said. "In fact, we just did a piece of work for the United States Government."

"Shut up, Sam," Slocum hissed.

The blonde tipped her head. "Oh, sure you did," she said disdainfully.

"No, really, we did," Sam said. "We brought in the Conrad brothers, and right now we're on our way to Carson City to—"

Slocum slipped a boot out of his stirrup and kicked Sam in the shin.

"Ouch!" Sam said through gritted teeth.

The women were already moving toward them through the deep brush, leading the limping bay behind them.

Too late.

Slocum growled, "You just keep your mouth closed, kid. I mean it. They ain't got no need to know our business. Understand?"

Sam reached down and gave his leg a good rub. "You don't have to go woundin' me again."

"I only kicked you in the leg, you idiot. One of those Conrads got your arm."

Sam rolled his eyes. "Gol-durn it anyhow!"

"Here they are," said Slocum. The women had emerged from the tangled growth and stood before them. Once again, he tipped his hat. "My name's Slocum," he said gruffly. "This child over here is Sam Biggle."

"Cut it out," Sam hissed.

"Howdy, fellers," said the little blonde. She was a dance-hall type, all right. He just couldn't figure out what she was doing with the brunette.

"I'm Patsy," the blonde went on. "Patsy Himmel." She poked a thumb toward her companion. "And this here's Mariah Clemm."

Sam swept his hat all the way off. "Pleased, ma'am," he replied, and Slocum could see that he had no eyes for anyone but Patsy.

Patsy giggled softly. "I'm sure," she said.

Mariah stood beside her, lips pursed. "You'll have to excuse my friend," she said to Slocum. "She's an idiot."

"And you're an old stick-in-the-mud, Mariah!" Patsy replied.

"Ladies, ladies!" said Sam as he swung down off his paint. "Let me take a look at your horse." He ground-tied his mount and made his way toward Patsy. There was no Mariah involved in it at all, Slocum observed. Sam was smitten.

Well, what the hell.

While Sam made a big show of checking the horse's hooves, Slocum leaned on his saddlehorn. "What happened?" he asked Mariah.

She looked up at him. Still with distrust on her face, but you know, she had the loveliest eyes! Deep, soft brown, with delicate brows. Now that he had a chance to look at her up close, he saw that she had a widow's peak too, making her altogether pleasant face appear heart-shaped. Pink and pouting lips and a neat, straight nose rounded out the picture.

She was actually almost a looker. A nice dress with some color to it and a smidgen of makeup, and she could pass for a real beauty.

"Do you always stare, sir?" she asked.

Slocum felt a little grin flicker across his face before

he consciously forced his features blank and said, "Right sorry if I was, ma'am. So what happened?"

She sniffed. "We were headed for Carson City. Miss Himmel has a job waiting for her at Hector Parson's dry goods. As for myself, I have been engaged to teach school."

Well, that sure made sense, didn't it? A schoolteacher.

"I see," said Slocum.

"We had purchased two horses," she continued, "but mine ran off some time back. We attempted to forge ahead with just the one, but as you can see . . ." She shrugged.

Just then, Sam piped up, "Yup, Slocum. It's a rock." He tossed it out, and it landed at Swampy's hooves in a little puff of dust. " 'Fraid you ladies ain't gonna be ridin' this old bay for a spell." He clapped the horse on the shoulder.

Next to him, Patsy clapped a hand to each cheek and tipped her head sadly. "Oh, pooh!"

"Something like that," Mariah added, staring back at Patsy. Slocum couldn't see Mariah's face. But then she turned toward him again. "I suppose we would be pleased to accept the offer you gentlemen have made us, Mr. Slocum. That was the name, correct?"

"Yes'm," he said. Pretty or not, she was a stiff little piece of work.

With a sigh, he swung down off the Appy, then led him, along with Sam's paint, over into the shade.

"Excuse me?" Mariah called. "Mr. Slocum? Aren't we going to be on our way?"

Slocum reached into Sam's saddlebags for the hobbles

and bent to put them on the paint. "No, ma'am," he said. "Not just yet."

He flicked his eyes toward her, and saw that she was standing there, hands balled into fists, with her face looking like she'd just had a mouthful of lemon juice straight up.

"If you mean to take advantage of this situation, sir, I should like to inform you that—"

"I'm only takin' advantage of a chance to rest these horses, ma'am," he said, and stood upright. As he slid the paint mare's saddle and bridle off, he added, "They're gonna be carryin' double, so you'll just have to get used to it. We're gonna be doin' a lot of stopping."

The paint taken care of, he moved to do the same for Swampy. He glanced up toward the sky. "In fact," he added, "I don't think we're gonna be doin' too much more in the way of travelin' today. We're about to lose the sun."

Mariah tapped her dainty foot. She turned her watch pin toward Slocum, as if he could read it from fifteen feet away.

"It's only four-thirty, Mr. Slocum," she said. "Don't play games with me. Surely there is sufficient time remaining before sunset to travel on for at least an hour and a half!"

"You ain't used to travelin' through the mountains too much, are you, honey?" he said, leaning on Swampy's saddle.

That "honey" ticked her off, all right, just as he'd meant it to. But although her face showed the sting, she didn't speak of it. Instead she just said, "That is beside the point, sir."

"No," he said, "that's exactly the point."

"Ma'am?" said Sam, who had just led the bay up. Patsy was practically glued to his hip. She seemed a little too friendly for a dry-goods clerk, if you asked Slocum. She was a little too friendly for a dance-hall girl!

Sam tipped his hat to Mariah and said, "See, when you're down in this pass, like we are, sunset comes a whole lot earlier than when you're on the flat."

Mariah flicked a distrusting eye toward Patsy. "Well?"

Patsy nodded. "That's right, Mariah. Double swear with a spit."

"Please don't use those vulgar expressions, dear," Mariah said wearily. She turned back toward Slocum, who was actually beginning to enjoy this, in a perverse sort of way.

"Very well, Mr. Slocum," she said. "I suppose I will have to take your word for it."

"Looks like it, don't it?" he said. He turned back to the business of getting Swampy hobbled and his tack stripped off. "And it's just Slocum," he added. "No Mister to it."

"And my name is Miss Clemm," she said right back. "There is no 'honey' to it."

Slocum let Swampy's saddle drop with a thump. Grandly, he swept off his hat. "Oh, yes, ma'am, Miss Clemm," he said with a full bow. "Whatever you say, Miss Clemm."

With worry in her voice, Patsy said, "Mariah, couldn't you just once be—"

Mariah ignored her. "You are very rude, Mr. Slocum," she said.

Slocum smiled at her. As he unbuckled Swampy's bridle, he said, "I can say the same for you, Miss Clemm."

Sam moved in between the verbal combatants. In his best peacemaker voice, he asked, "Have you ladies eaten yet? We got us some good fried chicken, cooked by the finest woman in the whole county, and I think there's more'n enough for everybody."

7

The sun had long since gone down, dinner had been eaten, and Sam had pulled out his harmonica. While he played the sweet sounds of an old Civil War ballad, "Lorena," the rapt women sat across the fire.

Not Slocum, though. He had left the scene early on to go stand watch, he had said. At the moment, he was about one hundred yards up the closest hill, the thin sound of the harmonica floating up to him, and the tiny figures of the listeners like specks about the fire as he kept watch.

So far things had been pretty dull, and he was grateful for that. He'd gotten a little lax about staring up and down the canyon, watching the dark brush and trees for any sign of movement, watching for little flashes of moonlight that weren't made by critters' eyes or lightning bugs.

He was, in fact, staring at Mariah. Miss Clemm to him.

He snorted. Now, what on earth had gotten a woman that pretty so all-fired righteous?

Maybe it was because she wasn't married yet. He figured she had to be in her late twenties. Or maybe she wasn't married because she was so goddamned high-and-mighty.

Hard to tell.

The blonde, Patsy, wasn't anything like her. She'd been practically permanently attached to Sam's arm since a half hour after they'd gotten down off their horses.

Not that Sam appeared to be upset about it.

He was down below, playing song after song on his harmonica, showing off for the women. Well, showing off for Patsy, that is. He'd barely noticed that Mariah was alive, except to whisper, "Pesky, ain't she?" at Slocum right after she'd let loose another load of vitriol.

Well, let Mariah keep her highfalutin airs, that was all Slocum had to say. He figured this was his little bow to being civilized, taking these two women down to Carson City. Maybe it balanced the fact that just two days ago, he'd killed three men. They were awful bad men, but men nonetheless.

He pulled out his fixings pouch and began to roll himself a quirlie.

Women, he thought as he gave a lick to the paper. *Can't live without 'em, can't . . .*

Well, he was sure there was something witty to say in there, but he couldn't think of it right at the moment.

He tucked away his fixings, stuck the quirlie between his lips, and was about to strike a match when he saw it and paused.

Just a spark of light, so tiny and quick that he could have imagined it.

It was up the pass a good ways, and up in the trees. Maybe somebody lighting a smoke, just as he'd been about to do.

You'd think that somebody camped that close would have seen their fire and hailed them, maybe come in for some grub and some company.

No, he'd just thought he'd seen something, that was all. But old habits died hard, and he watched the place in the darkness, watched it steady and long.

And saw another glimmer.

Somebody was there, all right. Somebody was sitting up there, watching their campsite and smoking a cigarette.

Slocum's brow furrowed. He forgot all about his unlit smoke and let it drop to the ground. Quietly, he rose and slid off through the trees.

Doolin Conrad wasn't happy, to say the least. He had ridden into the tiny Nevada town of Quicksand that afternoon, and had barely tied his horse to the rail when some idiot he'd never seen in his life told him his brothers were dead.

He'd hauled off and slugged the jabbermouth for his trouble.

Except that when he went into the saloon, the whole place was buzzing with it. All four of 'em, killed by some young wet-behind-the-ears shootist named Sam Biggle and the notorious Slocum. Folks said his brothers were murderers. Folks called Slocum and this upstart, Biggle, big heroes.

Doolin left and went back into the alley by himself, and waited until his face quit twitching and his eyes stopped watering, and until he could control the grief twisting his features. And then he went back inside and asked somebody where he could meet this famous Slocum and this stalwart Sam Biggle and shake their hands.

When they asked him his name, he told them Smith.

And so, he'd spent that afternoon riding hard toward Carson City, which meant toward Summit Pass. It wasn't that he loved his brothers. It wasn't even that he liked them, the crookedy-toothed, ugly little varmints. He'd ridden across their path completely by accident. Hadn't spoken to Arvil, Dread, Corbett, or Zeb for more than five years.

But they'd been his brothers, by God. He remembered them when they were little, all towheaded and sort of cute and getting under his feet. They'd been from his pa's second wife. The bitch. She'd shot out kids like a damned Gatling gun until she'd upped and died giving birth to the last one. Was that Arvil? No, it was Dread. He thought.

Didn't matter. He was a Conrad, and so had they been. It didn't matter what they had or hadn't done to deserve their deaths. Nobody killed his brothers and got away with it.

He had reached the pass—just the beginning of it, where the hills on either side were beginning to rise up almost imperceptibly—at sunset, and decided to camp. He knew he was on the right trail. He'd seen their tracks coming in.

But they weren't alone.

Another set of tracks, one horse carrying a lone rider, and a big one at that, had gone before the two that he assumed were Slocum and Biggle.

Another set, this one also a lone rider, had gone after.

And so now, sitting before his small fire and staring ahead, toward the vast expanse of canyon, he scratched at his head. Those folks in Quicksand were awful talkative. Without even asking, he'd learned that the reward on his brothers was eight thousand altogether, and that the bank in town couldn't handle the payment. He'd also learned the names of both his brothers' killers without asking.

A couple of simple questions, asked in passing of over-eager drunks, added the information that they were taking the pay voucher south, to Carson City.

And that they'd left this morning.

All that jabber and no one with sense enough to put a lid on it. Those other tracks he'd seen might belong to other fellows with something in their minds like the idea he had.

Of course, he thought, they'd be after the voucher. Maybe they'd leave those boys alive. He hoped so. At least, long enough for him to kill them.

Slocum slipped silently through the brush.

He'd gone the long way around, gone south far past his own fire, so as not to alert Sam Biggle and the two ladies that he was up to anything at all, that anything was amiss. Then he'd crossed the pass and headed north again, circling them.

And now, a good twenty minutes later, he was nearly to the place where he'd seen that cigarette glowing.

Quietly, slowly, he crept forward in a crouch, suffering constant stings and scrapes and sticks from the bush and bramble. Once he got his hands on this fellow, he figured to take every one of those stickers and nettles and spines out of his spying hide.

He heard a rustle up ahead, and sank down on his heels, holding his breath, listening.

And then he heard something that couldn't have been

caused by any deer or bear. It was the creak of saddle leather.

He leapt to his feet just in time for the rider to bowl him over.

The horse's shoulder collided with his. He swung out an arm as he fell, trying to get a handhold on something, anything. But the only thing he got was the tail end of the girth strap, and the horse's speed tore it from his grasp.

He listened from flat on the ground as the horse galloped away.

He pushed himself up on his elbows.

"Goddamn it," he muttered. "Sonofabitch!"

He stood up and brushed himself off, only then noticing that his hand was torn up from the leather strap. He couldn't see it through the darkness, but it stung like hell.

The sound of the horse's hooves had gone back up north instead of south, toward Sam and the girls. At least they were safe. So he walked forward a few feet until he came to the place where their watcher had made camp.

It didn't look like their visitor had planned to stay long. There was no sign of a fire. In the slim light, Slocum couldn't even find the man's cigarette butt.

"Slocum?"

Slocum's hand went to his gun automatically and he'd drawn it before he realized that the speaker was Sam.

He jammed the Colt back down and said, "Goddamn it, don't sneak up on me!"

Sam lowered the nose of the rifle he was holding on Slocum. "What the hoop-de-doodlin' hell you doin' out here anyhow?"

"Thought I saw somebody," Slocum replied as he

pushed past him, headed back down toward camp.

"And did you?" asked Sam, on his heels.

"Yeah."

"And?"

Slocum sighed and pushed a low branch from his path. "There was a feller. He took off before I could introduce myself."

That seemed to be enough explanation for Sam, because he didn't speak again all the way back to the fire.

8

In the quiet of the night, Mariah and Patsy clearly heard the ruckus up the canyon. They were already edgy, Sam having excused himself about fifteen minutes earlier. Giving a tip of his hat brim, he had silently melted back into the dark brush.

"Come on," Mariah said, and grabbed Patsy's arm.

"Why?" snapped Patsy. "It's probably just old Joe, takin' 'em out."

"Hush!" said Mariah, then whispered, "That wasn't the plan. And you know that Joe always sticks to the damned plan."

For better or worse, she added with a silent grimace. Dragging Patsy behind her, she moved back into the dark beyond the fire's light and behind the screen of a half-grown cypress.

"Mariah . . ." Patsy began in a whine.

"Shut up," Mariah said firmly. "Just shut up and watch."

Miraculously, Patsy did.

This was trouble. Not that Patsy was being quiet, but

her reason for it. If that truly was Joe out there, then Slocum or Sam must have spotted him. For all she knew, Joe could be lying out there, spilling his guts about the whole plan.

She caught herself worrying about what was going to happen to her, reminding herself that Joe was the one who might be in trouble right this minute, and that she and Patsy hadn't exactly done anything illegal.

Yet.

And then she mentally kicked herself for worrying about Joe. As if he ever bothered to worry about her. Or Patsy. No, it was just follow the plan, girls. Cut the purse, girls. Here's your lousy portion of the take, girls.

Some part of her rather hoped that they *had* caught him.

However, those hopes were dashed when Slocum and Sam came stalking back into the firelight.

Patsy rushed out from behind the tree and into the light, and threw her arms around Sam's neck. "Oh, Sam!" she cried. "I was so worried!"

"Don't overdo it, honey," Mariah muttered, and then she stepped out too. "Mr. Slocum?" she called, her voice and demeanor abruptly returning to the cold fish Slocum knew. "Are you injured?" She could see that there was something wrong with his hand, and was surprised when she felt something akin to actual concern.

Get a grip on yourself, Mariah, she thought. *He's just a mark.*

He didn't answer her, just knelt beside the fire and pulled a canteen from his pack. "You stand first watch," he said to Sam as he opened the canteen and poured water over his palm.

She could see it now that she was closer. Something

had stripped the flesh from his palm, something like a rope.

"Oh, dear!" she cried, and hurried the rest of the way toward him. "Here, let me."

She was dabbing the wound and pouring more water before she realized it. Patsy slid her a long look that said a number of things, primary, *Don't* you *screw this up, Miss High-and-Mighty.*

She heaved a little sigh, and Slocum said, "I can take care of it."

She looked up. She couldn't read his face. She said, "Nonsense. Have you any medical ointment?"

He looked at her strangely, as if she'd climbed down from some cloud somewhere. And then he reached for his pack again, and pulled out a little leather bag. One-handed, he opened it and pawed through its contents until he found what he was looking for.

He handed her a small metal tin. "This what you wanted?" he asked. She wasn't completely certain, but she was pretty sure there was a smile lurking just under his surface.

She tore her eyes away from his and read the printing on the tin. *Johnson's All Purpose Salve for Cuts, Bruises, and Superficial Wounds. Approved for Human and Live-stock Use,* it read. She wondered just who had "approved" it.

"This seems safe," she said anyway, and opened it. She began to dab it on the wound.

"Why?" he asked, the trace of a twinkle in his eye. " 'Cause it's safe for critters and folks alike?"

She forced her eyes away and stared pointedly at his

hand. "Something like that, Mr. Slocum. How did you receive this?"

"Leather strap," he said matter-of-factly. "Tried to get a handhold on a fella, and all I caught was his girth strap. Unfortunately, he was moving at the time. Didn't bother to stop either."

She put the lid back on the tin. "How careless of you."

"Some folks might say so," he replied.

She stood erect. "What have you for bandages, Mr. Slocum?"

"Oh, this is fine." He squinted at his hand. "Thanks. Now, you and Patsy had best—"

"Tut, tut, Mr. Slocum," she said in her best schoolteacher voice. "You'll sit right down and you'll not move until that wound is covered by a clean bandage." And when he just stood there, she folded her arms and added, "Now!"

He gave an amused shake to his head, but he sat down.

"One moment, please," she said. She turned her back and lifted her skirts, and began to tear off pieces of her petticoat.

"Can I help?" he asked.

She kept her back to him. "Mr. Slocum!" she said, and tried to make it sound as incensed as humanly possible. In truth, she found him most attractive. Now, wasn't that odd?

From behind her, his deep voice murmured, "That's just Slocum, Miss Clemm. If you please."

Gooseflesh swept her spine, and she nearly turned around just to make certain he wasn't standing right behind her, close enough to kiss. Part of her hoped he was.

But when she turned to face him again, he was still

sitting there patiently on his rock, waiting, holding out his hand.

She took a deep breath and quickly checked around for Patsy. The silly girl was nowhere in sight, blast her. She should have been there, if for nothing more than to chaperone. And suddenly, Mariah was feeling in dire need of a chaperone.

"Hold these, please," she said curtly, and placed all the cloth strips but one in Slocum's free hand. By the light of the flickering fire, she began to bind the wound. It looked worse than it was, she knew. He'd be using it fine again come tomorrow, although it was certainly going to be tender.

"If you found another gentleman camped up there," she said, staring at her work, "why didn't you invite him down for coffee? It would seem the civilized thing."

"Didn't hang around long enough for me to see if he was civilized or not," Slocum said softly. His face was inches from her bent head.

Mariah bit at her lip and took another cloth strip from Slocum. "You don't think he meant us harm, do you?"

"Can't rightly say."

She could feel his breath moving her hair, brushing the tendrils against her face.

"Will he come back, do you think?" she asked, but this time her voice broke.

"Sam and I'll watch," he whispered. "You won't come to any harm."

She raised her eyes to his, totally, absolutely mesmerized by his voice and the nearness of him. "Your hand," she said falteringly. "Your hand is—"

"Get the bandage done then?" said Patsy, stepping out

of the brush with all the finesse of a herd of elephants. Her hair was full of twigs and her clothing looked disheveled.

Mariah jerked alert, and Slocum stood up.

"Y-yes," Mariah said, and she was glad that the darkness disguised her flush. "He's all done."

"Oh, I ain't even started yet," Slocum said close to her ear, and so low that only she heard it. She flushed even more hotly.

"Good," said Patsy, oblivious. "I'm tired." Humming a gay tune, Patsy stepped around the fire and slumped down on her blankets. She pulled a hand mirror from her pack, and began to preen. "Nasty old twigs!" she muttered.

When Mariah felt safe to turn and face Slocum, he was sliding into the brush as easily as some wild thing. He was simply there one moment and gone the next, without so much as a word.

She stared after him for a moment, feeling a pang of longing. Or was it remorse? Frustration? Guilt?

She didn't know. And now wasn't the time to figure it out.

Just do your job, Mariah, she told herself. *Stop thinking wicked thoughts about a saddle tramp you barely know. Stop thinking about his hands, his eyes, and what he must be like in bed. You haven't had thoughts like this for years, haven't had feelings like this for even longer! What's wrong with you?*

Patsy stopped humming and looked up. "What on earth's the matter with you?" she asked. "You look all . . . all flustered or somethin'."

"Nonsense."

"He's getting to you, ain't he?" Patsy went on. She was

brushing her hair now, as if it would help. She must have half the trees for a mile around stuck in it. "Figure'd you fall for one of 'em someday, just didn't think it'd be on this trip. And didn't figure it'd be somebody like that saddle tramp."

Mariah scowled. "You're crazy."

Patsy smiled, and her brush never stopped moving. "I'm not crazy. I'm a gal who knows a good thing when she sees it. And I figure you are too."

"Just shut up, all right?"

Patsy said, "Honey, you can order me around all you want to. You can cuss and holler and carry on too, for all the good that'll do. Because when it comes to things between men and women, sometimes they're just gonna happen, whether you want 'em to or not. And that's the truth."

Shaking her head, Mariah went to her pallet and sat down. "As if you're an expert," she said snidely. "And just never you mind," she added. "Take care of your own business. I can take care of mine."

Staring at the fire, Mariah balled her hands into fists and repeated to herself, *Just do your damned job. Don't think about anything else, girl.*

Up the canyon, Joe Harper was laughing his ass off as he finally reined his chestnut to a halt. Why, he hadn't had so much fun since he'd laid the rail!

What a hoot!

He'd heard that polecat sneaking up on him, yes, he had. Heard a twig break. He'd been waiting for him, and he'd timed it just right.

And he'd bowled the bastard over, ass over teakettle!

He wished he could have hung around to see the expression on his face when that stupid saddle tramp—he wasn't too sure who it was, the old one or the young one—had managed to finally get up.

He bet there'd been a lot of cussing, though. He grinned.

He kept on walking his horse up the canyon, past the point where you could barely tell it was a canyon, until the chestnut's breathing had evened out and it wasn't sweating. And then he started to look for a place to camp. Out here, one place was as good as another, he guessed.

He was just about to halt his chestnut alongside a tall and lonely juniper when from nowhere, a shot rang out.

He didn't know that he was hit right away.

He just sat there, swaying in his saddle, and then he was vaguely aware that he was falling, that he had hit the ground.

Cheek down in the dirt, looking square at his horse's front hooves, he blinked. It crossed his mind that this wasn't fair, goddamn it.

Why, he was about to be a rich man!

And then the dim outline of his horse's hooves became even dimmer.

Joe tried to swallow, but couldn't.

All in a rush, he thought about Patsy and Mariah. He thought about before that, back with Eppie and the blue garter and those damned ducks of McQuade's, and even back before that, to Jasmine Jones.

He thought about all the cons he'd worked, and especially the ones that had worked out just the right way.

He thought about when he was a kid and his ma used

to make tomato gravy for special treats, and when he had a dog named Patches.

He thought about all this and more in the space of perhaps five seconds.

And then nothing.

Mariah sat up and tipped her head. Had she just imagined it?

"You hear something?" she whispered to Patsy, across the fire. "Sounded like a shot, far off. Or maybe a firecracker."

"Aw, go back to sleep," Patsy replied groggily, and pulled her blanket up over her head. "You're hearin' things. Firecrackers, my ass."

9

Up in the trees, Slocum heard it too. He stopped stock-still and waited for a second report, but none came.

He looked over at Sam and Sam looked at him. Sam broke the silence first. He shrugged, then said, "A celebration round, you reckon? I mean, for escapin' our clutches?"

Slocum furrowed his brow. "Hard to tell." He didn't know who had fired it, after all. It might have been their boy, the one who bowled him over up the canyon, or it might have been somebody else.

Slocum hoped it was somebody else. If somebody had fired at their mystery man, maybe that would spook him back this way. Slocum was more than eager to get his hands on him.

"Why we walkin' all over hell and gone?" Sam asked as he pushed another errant tree branch from his path. His arm appeared to be bothering him no longer, for he used it as freely as the other. "There ain't gonna be anybody else out here, Long-Tall." He let go of the branch too soon, and it slapped him in the face. He spat out a leaf.

"Nobody with any sense, that is," he said, and wiped his mouth.

Slocum knew he was right. At first, his anger at being hoodwinked by a bushwhacker had fired up his senses, and all he'd wanted to do was find another of the sonsofbitches and do himself a little getting even. He'd been embarrassed more than hurt, although his hand still throbbed beneath the fresh bandages, and he knew it would be good and sore tomorrow.

But now that the heat of the encounter had worn off a little, he could see the wisdom in what Sam said.

"All right," Slocum replied wearily. "You set your ass down right here and keep watch. Me, I'm gonna go up the canyon a little ways and do the same. You see anything, make an owl hoot. You can do that, can't you?"

By way of an answer, Sam cupped his hands over his mouth and did a prime imitation of a screech owl.

"That'll do," said Slocum, and trudged off up the canyon.

Doolin Conrad slipped out from his hiding place and walked toward the horse and the body. He was frowning, and his scowl grew deeper with every step.

"Goddamn it!" he snarled under his breath when he got within twenty feet. He'd been told in town that one of those murdering pipsqueaks rode a paint, and the other an Appy. He'd known right away that the galloping horse wasn't a paint, but he'd figured that it could be an Appy.

Just not a flashy one.

But by the time he'd walked within ten feet of it, he had to admit that nobody in their right mind would have considered the chestnut to be even a faintly marked snow-flake.

Shit and hellfire!

Here he'd gone and wasted a perfectly good bullet on the wrong fellow.

He didn't actually give up on the idea, though, until he'd rolled the body onto its back and gone through every pocket.

Joe Harper, that had been the fellow's name. Said so right there in his wallet, the one that was currently in Doolin Conrad's hand.

Damn and blast it!

He picked out what he wanted of Joe Harper's belongings, principally a nice pocketknife, thirteen dollars in silver, a pouch of pretty fair tobacco, and a picture of some gal, posed in skimpy dance-hall garb. He figured it would give him something to focus on when the trail got lonely at night.

The horse wasn't too much, and he figured it would be more work to lead it along behind than it was worth, so he stripped it of tack and swatted its rear. It seemed glad to go.

Then he dragged the body back into the brush and left it there. It was too much work to dig a damn hole for somebody he didn't even know. Plus which, the man wasn't exactly dead yet, though he would be by morning. Sooner, by the looks of it.

Hell, he'd probably be dead by the time Conrad walked back to camp!

Well, the buzzards would have that body picked clean in a few days anyway. He made sure to leave it faceup and rip open the shirt. Best to lure the scavengers in with the promise of fresh eyeballs and a direct route to the guts.

Then, grumbling as he walked, he trudged back up to where he'd camped, not 150 feet away, and rekindled his little fire. He'd put it out quick enough with a potful of coffee when he'd heard the approaching hoofbeats, just sloshed it out and run for the brush like the devil himself was on his tail. Now he had to collect fresh kindling—of which there wasn't all that much lying around—to get it going again.

And while he did, he was thinking what a god-awful rotten day this had turned out to be.

By about one-thirty, Sam had dozed off and shook himself awake again at least five times. He was presently stomping his feet, just to keep his mind on something besides sleep.

And Patsy Himmel.

He was sure attracted to that little gal. She reminded him a little of Elma Gimbal, a girl he'd gone to school with. Well, part of the way through school, because Elma quit when her daddy died after being kicked in the head by an ox. But Elma had been awful prim, even for a fifth-grader, and she didn't have that cute little upturned nose like Patsy did.

Or those nice titties.

Sam sighed. He should be down by the fire, talking Miss Patsy's ears full of honey, that's what he should be doing. Except that ol' Slocum had a bee in his bonnet about that fellow, and now everybody's night was ruined.

Hell, that man wasn't going to come back, not if he knew what was good for him! He'd taken off running like a true coward, hadn't he?

Sam figured that what he really ought to do was just go back down the hill and settle in. Preferably next to Patsy.

She sure had awful pretty hair. All floaty and curly. Fairy hair, his mama used to call it. And it was so blond! He wondered, did she have to put something on it to keep it that way, or did it come natural?

It didn't matter. He thought she was just fine. Oh, she was a little bit silly and a tad flighty, but weren't most gals?

She couldn't be nineteen, he figured. Maybe not even eighteen! That was pretty young for a gal to leave her mama and set off for a place like Carson City to take up a job in a dry-goods store.

He wondered if she had a mama. He hadn't asked.

He sighed, picked up a stick, and proceeded to dig list- lessly at the ground with it. Except that after a minute, he realized he was drawing those two big orbs that he imag- ined were inside the front of pretty Patsy's dress.

In the darkness, he flushed right up his neck to nearly his temples.

He tossed the stick away. Hell, he couldn't even trust his own hands!

But then he got to thinking about Patsy's front again. She had a fine little caboose too.

He stood up.

Hell, this wasn't getting him anyplace. Nobody was going to come back tonight. And he wanted more than anything just to go down to the fire and say hello to Patsy.

He'd say more, if she gave him a chance. He'd do more too.

He took a step, then paused. There was Slocum to think

about. Slocum would be pretty sore with him for deserting his post, so to speak. But then, Slocum was too antsy for his own good sometimes. Sam thought that he just might have to point that out.

And after all, Sam thought, he was young! Slocum was old. Well, practically middle-aged anyhow. And he probably didn't understand the call that a fine young woman sent out to a healthy young man.

Maybe too healthy for his own good, Sam reminded himself, and waited for the front of his trousers to get a little slack back in them.

Once that detail righted itself, he picked up his rifle and started back down the hill, into the pass, moving silently and eagerly toward the promise of Patsy.

What could it hurt?

About one hundred yards up the pass, Slocum was still berating himself for having been taken off guard. That sonofabitch must have known he was coming, that was all he could figure. He must have lit that smoke on purpose, figuring it would draw in any watchers. And Slocum had walked right into it, hadn't he?

But then, why in blue blazes would some traveler—be it thief or pilgrim—want to lure in a fellow, just to ride over the top of him and gallop off the other way? Could it have been some shy saddle tramp, too afraid to come in?

It just didn't make any sense.

While he was going over and over this enigma in his head, he noticed a little movement down the canyon, not too far from where he'd left Sam.

Brow furrowed, he pulled out his spyglass. There was

some moon but not much, but he was able to pick the kid out when he passed between two trees. Now, what was he up to?

Maybe moving down closer, so that he could keep an eye on the girls.

Maybe not.

But he hadn't made his signal, and so Slocum just sat and waited, sucking on his teeth.

That Mariah! Now, there was a little pisser. She was surely pretty, and she had the body of a plump angel, but glory be, that attitude! He'd like to wander on back down to camp and set her straight about a few things, that's what he'd like to do. He'd like to show her a few other things too.

He'd like to show her that there was more fun to be had than what came at church socials, more joy to be had than could come from teaching the first-grade primer, and better times to be had than sleeping all by her lonesome on some rough cot that the town had donated for the schoolmarm.

Yessir, he'd like to show her that, and a whole lot more.

Except that she wouldn't let a fellow get near her. Of that, he was pretty certain. She sure had a real big stick crammed up her ass.

He remembered to look for Sam again just as his shadowy figure appeared at the edge of the ring of firelight that was their camp.

"Why, you horny little bastard," Slocum muttered as he watched Sam sit down next to a blanketed figure and sort of "accidentally" nudge her awake.

Slocum knew this game. He'd invented it. And he folded his spyglass to give them some privacy.

Hell, he thought with an amused shake of his head. That Sam was some kind of bird dog, wasn't he?

Slocum turned his head away, his eyes searching up the pass. Sam should have stayed put, but Slocum figured that what with the call of Sam's hormones pretty much being at their peak—and the reason for his staying out there in the bushes being only important to Slocum—Sam was sort of entitled.

Slocum supposed that he would have done much the same thing at the kid's age, if the only reason he was standing guard was to make some fussy old saddle tramp happy.

Some old saddle tramp.

Now that was pathetic, wasn't it?

Slocum blew air out through pursed lips and stared up the pass. That was him, pathetic old Slocum, all covered in age and legend, fairly dripping with it, and sitting out here feeling sorry for himself.

Not just because some bushwhacker had gotten the drop on him, but because he'd let it happen.

And because Sam was down there by that fire, probably thinking about doing what Slocum himself should have been doing.

And because that damned Mariah was such a cold fish.

Aw, hell.

10

"Patsy?" Sam whispered. He was lying smack next to her beside the dying campfire, and that old biddy, Mariah, was across the way, dead to the world. He was surprised she wasn't snoring.

"Miss Patsy?" he repeated, and gave her a little shake.

Her eyelids fluttered a bit. "What's that?" she said, all soft and slurry. "Who's that?"

"It's me. Sam." This time he put his lips right up to her ear.

Good gravy, but her hair smelled pretty! Like lemons and such, all tart and sweet at the same time. "Are you awake, Patsy?"

And then her lips curled into a sleepy smile and her eyes opened just a touch. "Sam, honey? Is that you?"

He grinned. "Sure is, sugar pie."

She rolled toward him, and her hand came up to trace the line of his jaw. "I thought you were out on guard, darlin'," she said, and yawned. "What you doin' back here?"

"Aw, hell," he said. "There ain't nothin' or nobody

gonna come after us tonight. Slocum's just all het up cause that damned hombre got the drop on him. I figured I'd come on down and spend some time with you instead."

She smiled at him, and his heart nearly thumped out of his chest.

Now it wasn't that Sam wasn't worldly. He was. But the ways of women were, for him, restricted to the ways of the gals at the dance halls and whorehouses he frequented. He hadn't spent much time with real women, not women who were going to be clerks in a dry-goods store. This was a whole new thing for him. And he was wondering if maybe Miss Patsy Himmel wasn't just the right sort to move with him onto that ranch: the imaginary ranch with the imaginary cabin for two.

He was going to be fairly rich as soon as they hit Carson City, after all. Maybe God was just handing him his future in one package, sort of like, *Here you go, Sam. Now you've got a wife, a stake, and My blessings. Go in peace.*

Of course, he couldn't imagine what he'd ever done to deserve such a divine gift, but he wasn't going to ask any questions, no, sir!

"Well?" she said. "Here I am."

"I was wonderin', Miss Patsy . . . that is . . . could I mayhap give you a kiss?" He flushed when he said it, and was glad he was in between the fire and her. Maybe she hadn't seen.

He guessed she hadn't, because she smiled, all sort of come-hitherish, but sweet just the same, and whispered, "I reckon you could, Sam, if you're of a mind."

He gave a quick nod. "I am."

She closed her eyes and puckered her lips.

Well, you didn't have to ask Sam twice.

He leaned forward and kissed her, real gentle and soft, and when he was done, she opened her eyes and murmured, "Why, that was sure awful nice, Sam. Would you do it again?"

Across the fire, Mariah squirmed down into her blankets. Oh, that little she-idiot! Imagine, Patsy feigning innocence! Well, it was part of the scam, she supposed. It was just that Patsy was so bad at it.

And innocent, Mariah's foot! Why, Joe told her he'd picked up Patsy down in the border country. Went into a cantina, he'd said, and there was Patsy, stripped stark naked except for her shabby jewelry and her high-heeled shoes, prancing around the floor from customer to customer and bending over the tables for anybody with a couple of pesos in his pants.

Even Joe had been a little bit disgusted.

And Joe, being so jaded, was pretty damned hard to disgust.

And listen to her! "That sure was nice, Sam. Do it again?"

Mariah snorted in spite of herself, and then held very still hoping the noise hadn't alerted them to her wakefulness.

It hadn't. They were past the point of noticing much of anything. The sounds of heavy breathing came to her ears, and she rolled her eyes.

Except that all that heavy breathing and the smacking sounds of their lips were having another effect on her. Namely, that her nether parts felt nearly on fire.

Stop it, Mariah! she told herself. *This is just plain silly!*

She tried not to listen, jammed her fingers in her ears beneath the blankets, and tried to sleep.

She didn't have much luck.

"You'll go easy, Sam?" Patsy was whispering into his ear. "You won't hurt me?"

"I promise," Sam said. He'd had second thoughts about this—about deflowering her right out here in the open, in front of God and everybody—but they were fleeting. Patsy was the one, yes, sir. Plus which, he was about to poke a big old hole right through the front of his britches.

"I'd never hurt you, Patsy, honey," he whispered, and kissed her temple. "Why don't you just unbutton my britches, darlin'? Just unbutton 'em and reach inside."

"Oh, Sam!" she said, and her voice was full of blushes. "You want me to touch you?" Against his chest, she gave a little shudder. "There?"

"It's all right, Patsy," he murmured. "It won't bite."

"But I never . . ."

He kissed her again. She was kissing him back better each time. Why, just a few more kisses and she'd kiss as good as any eager whore! And then he felt bad, comparing her to a soiled dove and all.

He didn't feel bad long, though, because right then her dainty hand snaked down between them, and he felt the pressure of her fingers against his crotch. Boy, just that little touch almost set him off!

He broke off the kiss long enough to whisper, "Mayhap I'd best do it, Patsy."

Except that when he reached down for the first button, he kind of had to fight her for it. Funny. But you never could tell about virgins, he guessed. Some of 'em were just born to it and some weren't. He was glad he had a gal that was going to like it.

"You'll be quiet, won't you?" she whispered. "I don't want to go waking Mariah. Oh she'd be so angry! She doesn't believe in—"

Just then he freed himself from the prison of his britches and placed her hand upon him.

"Oh, my!" she hissed, and her eyes grew large.

Gosh, but she was sweet!

"It's all right, Patsy," he whispered, soothing her. "It's gonna be fine. Just relax and let it happen."

"W-what are you going to do with that . . . that thing?" she asked.

He chuckled. "That ain't no 'thing,' honey. It's my John Henry."

Slowly, he worked her skirts up under the blanket.

"I'm gonna show you, baby doll, gonna show you real easy. Now kiss me again."

Mariah, scant feet away but long forgotten by Sam and Patsy, wormed her hand south under the blankets, toward her crotch. God damn them anyhow! That she should have to resort to this at her age! And that she should have to be so careful about it, so that they wouldn't see!

Criminy!

But her insides were aching something fierce, and she was so twitchy that she had to do something about it. If she didn't, she swore she'd lose her mind.

Slowly, carefully, she inched up her skirts.

•   •   •

Patsy's skirt was pooled around her waist, and he had her blouse open. Man, oh, man, and what beauties her titties were! She'd fought him a tad when he'd tried to ease the blanket down so that he could see them, but a long kiss had eased her mind quick enough.

Oh, they were round and white and so big, with rosy nipples that were hard with want, and puckered to greet only him. There really was something special about seeing tits that no fellow had ever seen before, wasn't there?

He bent his head and took one pretty nipple into his mouth, and Patsy gave out a little moan.

"That's right, baby doll," he whispered, his head to her breast. "Just let yourself go with it. Your Sam's here. He'll fix everything."

He slid one hand down over her belly to touch her little hairy place, then slipped his fingers lower. Boy howdy, she was as wet and slippery as pond weeds, and the moment he touched that moisture, he felt himself about to go right over the edge.

Hold on there, Sam, he told himself. *Just hold up. You got a lot longer to wait.*

He got himself calmed down a mite, and by then she had spread her legs. Funny. Well, mayhap that just came natural to gals. After all, their bodies were made for it, weren't they? He didn't have to think about it at all to know where he was supposed to put it, not even the first time.

Maybe gals were the same way about things such as that.

He moved then, moved over betwixt her legs, and eased his way inside her.

She gasped when he did, and he had to cover her mouth

with his hand. "Shh, honey," he whispered. "We don't wanna wake anybody, do we?"

She shook her head, and he slowly pushed the rest of the way inside.

Oh, but she felt so good! All warm and wet and hugging him tight between those soft and silky walls of hers. And she looked like she was enjoying it too. At least, her eyes were half lidded and her parted lips were curled up into a soft little smile.

He ducked his head and kissed her again, long and slow and soft, and then he asked, "Are you ready, sweet pea?"

Her lashes fluttered, and then she looked up at him. "I am, darlin'," she said. "I am."

11

Slocum stood up and silently shook out his legs, one at a time. There was still no movement out there, no man-made sound, no spark or glowing ember to show a man's position.

Frankly, he was about to just quit and go back down to the fire. At least he could get a hot cup of coffee. There wasn't anybody lurking out there, no matter how stirred up he'd been before. That sneaky sonofabitch had lit out, and lit out hard.

Hell, the bastard was probably halfway to Canada by now!

He sure hadn't wandered back this way. That was for sure.

Course, Slocum hadn't checked the camp lately, fig-uring to give that Patsy and ol' Sam a little privacy. Well, as much privacy as they could get, out here in the open, and with *Miss* Marian Clemm about two feet away from them. Sam had better hope that Mariah was a real sound sleeper.

He peered down the pass. Sure enough, there they were,

going at it like two minks in high season. And there was Mariah, sleeping right smack next to them, right across the fire. He pulled out his spyglass and trained it on her. Eyes closed. Sleeping like a baby.

Except . . . There, he saw it again!

The little minx was awake. Her eyes blinked, then stared, then closed again. Her arms were both tucked inside that blanket, in which she was wrapped tighter than a bedbug, but did he see some movement?

Grinning, he leaned farther forward and slowly swept the spyglass down the length of her body.

By God, yes, there it was!

It seemed that their little Miss Mariah Clemm wasn't so high-and-mighty pure-D proper as she put on, was she? Lying there, pretending to be asleep, when all the time she was diddling herself in time with those two kids across the fire.

He laughed in spite of himself, and then stopped abruptly when it came to him that he was hard. Sonofabitch! Now that beat everything, didn't it? Hard as a rock, and all on account of that prim little vixen working herself.

Oh, he was crazy, that's what! Out of all the gals in the world, he had to pass up all the gals who actually wanted him and go and get a big old hard-on for Mariah Clemm: the girl least likely to spread her legs for him. The least likely to spread her legs for any man!

In something akin to disgust—but not quite—he collapsed the spyglass and sat there, drumming its cylinder against his thigh.

He turned and faced away from camp. Sitting there, looking at what was going on, wasn't going to get him calmed down any, no matter how far away it was.

To take his mind off it as best he could, he mentally started going through poker hands. One of a kind. One pair . . .

Sam was driving harder now, losing himself in it, forgetting that he should go easy, forgetting everything. Besides, Patsy seemed like a real natural and then some. Know just what to do and when to do it, by God. And those inside muscles of hers! Why, they were trained like she'd been born to this, like she'd been practicing just for him!

He felt himself racing toward the brink, and thought that he should hold up, he should slow down, that she wasn't ready. But it was too late. He couldn't stop himself now.

What had been a maddening itch in his loins burst into a bonfire that spread quickly out through his limbs, and as it did, he felt her buck beneath him.

The joy he took in Patsy's release fair to doubled his pleasure, and when he opened his eyes again, he caught just a last grimace as she finished her climax.

He grinned down at her.

"How was it, honey pie? You all right?" he asked as he smoothed one of those fairy curls away from her face. "I swan, I never met a gal it came so natural to!"

Panting, she smiled up at him. "Oh, Sam, is it always like this?" she whispered.

He thought fast. He had just about convinced himself that he was going to marry this girl—once he got his money, that is—and he didn't want her thinking that just any old farmer could make her feel the way he just had.

Hell.

He said, "Patsy, honey, I'm sorry to tell you, but it ain't. But sometimes, a man and a woman come together who have parts built just the right way. I reckon that we're just one of them happy accidents. It's fate, darlin'."

She blinked and smiled up at him. "Really, Sam? I never felt anything like that before. It was like . . . like . . . lightnin' in a bottle!"

"Don't reckon I've ever heard it put that way before, darlin'," he said, "but that just about says it all."

She threw her arms around him and hugged him close, and those big, pillowy breasts went squish against him. It sure felt nice.

And then, from across the fire, Mariah let out a sort of strange sound, kind of a strangled sigh. Sam twisted toward her. "Is she all right, you think?" he asked Patsy.

Patsy turned him back toward her and away from Mariah. "Oh, she'll be fine," she said. "She just chatters in her sleep sometimes." She stroked Sam's cheek. "You know, I didn't think I'd like kissin' a feller with a mustache, but I guess I like it just fine. And, of course, all the extra trimmings that went with it."

Sam felt himself blush right down to his toes. "You do, honey?"

Patsy's lashes fluttered. "Yes, I do. In fact, I like it so much . . ." She looked away for a moment, then turned her head back toward him. "Sam?"

"Yes, darlin'?"

"Do it again?"

Hoop-de-doodle!

He kissed her square on the lips. "You sure we won't wake her up?"

"Wake up who?" asked Patsy. She nibbled on his ear.

"Mariah." He felt himself getting hard again, and he was prouder than a peacock. He nuzzled the curve of her throat.

As he moved down to nibble at her breast, she replied, "No, I don't think she'll wake up any more than she did last time, sugar."

Right then, Mariah grunted and tugged the blanket over her head. In her sleep, Sam supposed. Funny that she should pick that exact time to do it, though.

Patsy put her hands on either side of his face, and whispered, "Sammy, honey? Can people do it other ways too? I mean, does it always need the feller on top?"

He grinned. "Honey, there are all kinds'a ways to do it."

"Show me?"

Under the covers, Mariah put her fingers in her ears. Oh, she'd kill that damned Patsy once they were alone together.

Oh, Sammy, is it always like this?

Christ, she could just vomit!

Did Patsy have no shame?

Probably not. *She* probably didn't have any either. Just two gals trying to make a living any way they could.

Mariah sighed. The minute Joe gave over her cut, she was leaving. Bye-bye Joe and Patsy, hello the green woods of Ohio. It was the only thing that kept her going.

And she wondered if Slocum was still sitting up there all handsome and steely, waiting for a Joe Harper that was too smart for him, a Joe Harper that had gone to ground.

At least for the night.

But tomorrow would be different. Tomorrow, Joe was supposed to signal them, just to let them know he was there. He'd said that he would make a curlew's cry at around noon.

Now, Mariah had debated this with him. First off, she wasn't so certain that there were curlews in Nevada. Joe had said of course there weren't, that's how she and Patsy would know it was him.

Patsy had laughed her ass off at that one, all right. Stupid Mariah, Patsy had said, always overlooking the obvious.

Except Mariah didn't think she was that stupid, not really. If these boys—Slocum especially—heard something that wasn't supposed to be there, why, Slocum would probably stop them right where they were and spread a one-man net out over hell and gone.

Slocum, she was especially certain, wasn't the slightest bit stupid.

The noise from across the fire was even louder than before. Young lovers in rut—or so poor Sam probably thought. Mariah actually felt a little sorry for him.

Oh, well. Some things just couldn't be helped.

For instance, a girl taking care of herself when faced with overwhelming sexual circumstances. At least she felt a little better now.

And so, Mariah shoved her fingers a little deeper into her ears and tried to sleep.

Slocum figured he'd given Sam and Patsy enough time, and turned around slowly. He was sitting on a big old granite boulder, and it had about put his backside to sleep.

The fire had died down some, and he couldn't see as well as he had before, but when he put the spyglass to his eye, he found Sam and Patsy going at it just as enthusiastically as before. Christ, didn't that Sam wear out? Didn't he know they had to be on the trail first thing in the morning? And come to think of it, why had Sam deserted his post?

Well, that was a little harsh. Slocum hadn't been mad at him for doing it before, so why should he be now?

It was just getting to him, that was all. First being overtaken by that goddamn bushwhacker, and now sitting up here with no company but bats and owls and the like, and watching Sam have him some fun at a distance.

Damn it.

If it weren't for that voucher in Sam's pocket, Slocum would have just climbed on his horse and ridden out and the hell with them. He'd find that bushwhacker and give him a taste of his own medicine.

Probably just some drifter with nothing else to do, or a kid out for some tomfoolery. Somebody ought to paddle him, that's what they ought to do. A visit to the woodshed, that's what was needed, and Slocum was the man who could haul his ass in there and apply the strap.

Frowning, he peered through the spyglass again.

They were still at it.

Even Mariah had stilled—grimly he hoped she'd had herself a good time—and was lying quietly on the other side of the dying fire, her blankets pulled over her head.

"Trying not to listen, *Miss* Clemm?" he muttered. He knew just how she felt.

Finally, he folded up the spyglass and put it away. Those two were going to be at it all night, by the looks of things. And hell, he figured that he and a vast assortment of women had made enough rowdy-dow by the light of too many campfires to mention. It was somebody else's turn, he supposed.

And nobody was coming. Whoever their visitor had been, he was long gone by now. Didn't mean he wouldn't turn up in the morning, but tonight, Slocum had a feeling that they wouldn't be bothered.

However, just in case, he stood up and moved to the ground, to a place where he could sit up against a big old tree trunk, and made himself as comfortable as he could.

He pulled Jeb Masterson's silver flask from his pocket, took a long sip, then replaced it firmly. It was mighty good bourbon, all right. He took just enough to settle him. Then he tilted his hat down over his eyes, crossed his arms, geared his ears up into listening mode, and tried to catch a few winks.

Up the canyon, Doolin Conrad was having a hard time sleeping. Not because of the man he'd just killed, for indeed he'd decided the man was dead, had to be by now. Not because of Slocum and Sam, or even his deceased brothers, Arvil, Dread, Corbett, and Zeb. No, none of them were bothering him in the least.

He couldn't sleep because his brain was twitching again.

This really pissed him off, this twitching-brain business. Doolin Conrad was a man who liked things plain and simple. You were either here or you were there, you were on your horse or you weren't, you were dead or you were alive, and mostly, you were asleep or you weren't.

It was the last one that gave him fits. Sometimes, he

settled right into a dreamless sleep that wasn't broken until dawn, when his bladder woke him. But nights like tonight, when he was disturbed, he just couldn't settle back into it. Neither could he quite wake up all the way. He seemed to get lost in some sort of twilight place where his dreams were many and often frightening, and from which he couldn't wake.

He was aware, though, aware of his dreams, of where he was in reality.

It was downright annoying.

Actually, it was terrifying, a fact that Doolin would not have admitted to anybody.

Right at the moment, he was being chased by a crocodile, right down the main street of Las Cruces, New Mexico. The immutable fact that he had never seen a real crocodile, much less been chased by one, was immaterial.

The fact was, that croc was chasing him, snapping those gigantic jaws on the cuffs of Doolin's britches, and running just as fast as Doolin himself. Now, Doolin knew it was a dream, was absolutely convinced of it. But that didn't stop him from feeling terror—the kind that turned your insides to mush and made your knees feel like jelly.

He kept telling himself to just turn around, turn around and face the damned lizard, because then it would turn into a cow or a dog or something. They always did, the things that chased him.

Of course, the dog or cow often changed again, into something even spookier.

And rather than face that cow or dog and whatever they were going to turn into—and then the spooky critter into which they'd metamorphose—Doolin, in his dream, just kept on running.

12

Slocum woke up as cramped as if he'd spent the night in a steamer trunk. Pale light was sending soft fingers through the trees as he creakily got to his feet. He stood there, bent over, holding on to the nearest trunk until his legs stopped cramping, then slowly stood up.

"Jesus," he whispered as he worked the kinks out of his neck. He was getting far too long in the tooth for sleeping against a tree. Even when he slept on the ground, in a place with no rocks—a rare find out here—it still took his body a lot longer to wake up than it took his brain.

He would have traded it in for a nice feather bed somewhere. He'd tried it, in fact, over and over. But by the third day, the call of the trail always made him forget about waking up out here and the pain that came with it. Those times, he only remembered the way the skies looked at night, and the morning star. He remembered the soft calls of doves at dawn and the little peeps that families of quail made as they scurried through the brush. He remembered the scent of juniper and creosote bush, and wild cherry trees, and the smell of a fire made with mesquite wood.

That is, until he got back out here. Then it was just birds and trees to him. And they were mostly in his way.

He started down toward the campsite, hoping that somebody would wake up by the time he got there and set the coffee on the fire. No, forget that. He hoped they would have the sense to make a fresh pot.

By the time he made his way up the pass and down to the camp, everybody was up. Good thing, because he sure didn't want to be the one to wake up those lovebirds. It was kind of embarrassing when it was somebody besides him caught in a compromising position.

Mariah heard him coming.

"Good morning, Mr. Slocum," she said, all business, as he walked into the open. She must have read his mind, because the next thing out of her mouth was, "Coffee will be ready soon."

He nodded and gave a grunt, and walked right past her—and right past Sam and Patsy—to the horses. He heard Sam scrambling to get up and follow him.

Slocum was measuring out Swampy's oats when Sam caught him up.

"Mornin', ol' Long-Tall!" Sam said, as spry as you please. The young should all be shot, Slocum thought. They all just stood right up after a night on the ground, like their bones didn't hurt.

Slocum stuck the oat bag under his arm and fastened the feed bag over Swampy's muzzle. The horse ground the grain happily.

He said, "So, how was your night in the trees? See anything?"

Sam had the good sense to color, and Slocum grunted again.

When Sam didn't answer, Slocum added, "I reckon that Patsy's a nice enough gal."

This brought a quick response. Sam nodded his head eagerly. "Oh, she sure is, she sure is!"

"You check your pockets, made sure you got up with everything you laid down with?"

Sam jerked his head back and looked puzzled, and then offended. "Say!"

Slocum didn't react. He only said, "Just for my peace'a mind, I'd appreciate it if you checked to make certain you still got that paper. I'd feel like a pure idiot if we were to ride in there all full of demands with nothing to back it up."

Sam's offended expression had slowly turned to one of fear. He slapped at his pockets, then closed his eyes and sighed. He reached in and pulled out the voucher, still folded neatly. "You're crazy, Slocum," he whispered, with a glance back toward the women. "Patsy ain't like that."

"Well, now, I'm sorry to be so suspicious, Sam," Slocum said as he began to curry the horse. "I mean, you having known her so long and everything. My apologies."

Sam opened his mouth, then closed it, then slowly broke out into a smile. "Aw, you're funnin' me, ain't you?"

Slocum stopped his brush and studied it for a second. "Yeah. But I can remember a few times I got stuff swiped off me by a pretty gal I'd just met. By a few I'd known awhile too."

Sam shoved the paper toward him. "You carry it then."

"Nope. You got it, you keep it. Just a word to the wise, Sam." He went back to currying Swampy again.

Sam shoved the voucher back into his pocket and shook his head. "You beat everything, you know that, Slocum?"

Slocum nodded. "Been told."

"Well, they was right."

At the call of, "Coffee, gentlemen?" they both turned toward the fire.

Mariah was walking toward them with two steaming mugs. She had traded that ugly dress she'd worn yesterday for a frock of pale yellow. It did wonders for her hair, which had been pretty to begin with, and there was a pin that looked like a cluster of fat ladybugs stuck in it on one side.

Mariah was a damn fine-looking woman, even first thing in the morning, Slocum thought. Especially fine-looking for somebody who'd had to lie there listening to Sam and Patsy rut the night away.

He said, "Thank you, ma'am," and took a cup. He smiled.

"You're welcome," she said. No fanfare, no "good morning," no eye contact or return of his grin, only the barest admission that Slocum was even there. She handed Sam his mug, then turned away.

"Ain't much one for conversation, is she?" Sam said philosophically.

Slocum sighed. "Reckon not," he said, and took the first sip of his brew. Hell. It was going to be a long, long day.

At half past noon, Mariah was beginning to grow a little skittish. Joe Harper was supposed to give them a sign at midday, but there had been nothing.

And it wasn't as if she couldn't hear him if he signaled. They had stopped for the midday meal, so there was no clatter and swish of hooves on the trail. Sam and Patsy were off someplace, doing things lovers did. Slocum was sitting in the shade about fifteen feet off, hat over his eyes, taking a nap.

Or pretending to nap.

All morning Slocum had been on the alert, twisting his head at every rustle of the brush he heard and some that he didn't.

They had led the bay gelding, who was still lame, behind them. Patsy had ridden behind Sam, leading the way, and Mariah had ridden behind Slocum. But while Patsy's and Sam's ride had been full of giggles and soft mutters and blushes and wandering hands, Mariah's ride behind Slocum's saddle had been a study in frustration.

Mariah didn't know what had come over her. The scent of him and the feel of him, all those hard angles and muscles under her hands, and just the idea of him—all solid and straightforward, manly and deep-voiced, honest and tough, not like Joe Harper at all—had gotten her a great deal more excited than she'd counted on.

By the time they made a stop for lunch—not just one of those quick stops to rest the horses, which were bad enough—she was ready to throw Slocum to the ground and have her way with him.

She hadn't, of course.

It had used up every ounce of will she had, but she'd managed to feign indifference to him. Briskly, she had excused herself, gone behind the bushes, sat straight down, and put her head in her hands.

She didn't know how much longer she could stand this.

Fortunately, it wouldn't have to be much longer. Joe would signal them, and then she could begin to warm up to Slocum. Not too much, just enough to keep him interested and intrigued.

By the time they got to Carson City, the plan was to have Slocum wound as tight as a two-dollar watch. She would "give in" and then rob him of his bounty money at the hotel. Of course, with Joe to watch her back. Watch her back? That was a good one. She figured he'd be downstairs at the bar, drinking his way through the money she was most probably risking her life to steal.

Patsy was supposed to do the same as Mariah. That is, just tease Sam until they got to Carson City. But, well, that was Patsy for you. No self-control.

Mariah supposed it was safe to just let her go with Sam. There was no way Mariah could have stopped her, when it came right down to it. But Sam seemed to Mariah like the sort that would be easily taken in. He wouldn't be likely to dump Patsy as used goods the minute they hit Carson City.

Frankly, Sam had the look of a man in love about him.

Strangely enough, Mariah found herself concerned about this. It wasn't that she particularly liked Sam. Or was it?

She shook her head. No. It was just that after so many years of taking men every way from Sunday—taking them for their week's pay or their life savings and everything in between—she was going a tad soft.

It was different, or at least she told herself so, with the others. You couldn't bilk a man who didn't want to be bilked, who wasn't trying to get something for nothing. That's what Joe said anyhow.

But Sam was so bloody trusting!

And what they were planning to do to Sam and Slocum wasn't bilking. And although there was certainly misrepresentation involved, it wasn't even a con, it wasn't even sporting.

It was more like out-and-out theft.

13

Doolin Conrad was a good thirteen years older than his closest half brother—late half brother, that is—and more than twenty the senior of the youngest.

It wasn't that Doolin's ma hadn't spat out kids like eels down a chute. She had. But none of them had lived past the age of two except for Doolin. There had been a whole cemetery full of them out back of the cabin, all with tiny little headstones, and flowers laid out on their birthdays.

His ma had been real fussy about that, and about keeping up the family plot.

It had always given him the willies, thinking about that lot full of dead babies, dead brothers and sisters, outside his bedroom window. The wind through the trees always sounded like whispers, and sent him ducking under the covers.

Not that he'd admit it.

After his ma died, his pa had let the lot grow wild. No more flowers, no more trimmed grass. And two years after he'd taken another to wife—that being thirteen-year-old Wanda Louise Kettle, the eventual dam of Doolin's four half brothers—his pa had pulled up the gravestones and put the whole field to cane.

Sentimental, Doolin's pa was not.

Course, neither was Doolin. But he thought about what his pa had done now and again, and it kind of pissed him off.

Not so much that he'd pulled the headstones off those little dead babies' graves, but that Doolin's own mama had been in one of them.

It just didn't seem fitting.

And now, all these years later as he ambled down Summit Pass behind Slocum and Sam, he started to think about it again. And he wondered what Arvil, Dread, Corbett, and Zeb had done with his pa's body.

He sort of hoped they'd just tossed it down the holler to rot. It would have served the old bastard right, having his eyeballs pecked by birds and his innards invaded by slithery things.

Doolin hadn't used the old man's name in years. Couldn't stand for anybody to call him Conrad, on account of he always looked behind him to see if they were addressing his pa. And he didn't like the idea that his pa was always in back of him, even if only in spirit.

So he'd changed his name. Changed it a few times, to tell the truth. Changed it every time the one he was currently using got a little too well-worn or familiar to the authorities.

Although he'd been "Smith" back in Quicksand, right now he was "Doolin Cash." He'd gone back to his original first name, seeing as how using the first name of Garth had nearly gotten him killed up in Montana, because he forgot that he was Garth, and therefore he didn't

duck when old Chili Yeager hollered, "Garth! Look out!"
And he'd only used Smith in town because the first fellow
that asked took him off guard, and he forgot that he was
supposed to be a Cash.

But anyway, now it was Doolin again. That was probably safe. At least he could remember it, and he hadn't
used Doolin for about ten years. To tell the truth, he probably would have gone back to using the Conrad part
again, except for those jackass half brothers of his.

There was paper up on them in practically every town
big enough to own a jail cell. Some that didn't have jails
too. There they stuck them up in the post office or the
dry-goods.

Frankly, he'd rather have fouled his name all by
himself, thank you. But those idiot boys . . .

So Doolin Cash it was. He figured if somebody yelled
"Doolin!" at him, it would get his attention pretty damn
quick. Ditto the Cash part. He'd always been one to look
up at the mention of money.

And he thought it was particularly fitting, what with
Slocum and Sam Biggle on their way to Carson City to
collect the cash reward on his half brothers. Hell, he'd
collect it himself. Sort of a legacy, you might say.

Now the trail had gotten sort of interesting. Three
horses instead of two, all traveling together. Nobody was
riding the third horse, but the first two seemed to be carrying a double load. And when he'd checked the place
where they'd camped for the night, he'd found a lady's
hairpin.

So maybe that extra weight on the horses was women.
Two women.

He didn't much care where those females had come

from, but he was glad they'd shown up. He figured they'd come in handy. That much more diversion with the shooting got under way, that much more for Slocum and Sam to worry about.

Not that he planned on having Slocum around for much of it. Hopefully, none of it. He planned to take out Slocum right off the bat. Maybe hide somewhere and just pick him off.

It seemed the most likely choice. He'd heard of Slocum, all right, and even though he was still mad about Slocum and Sam killing his half brothers, he wasn't *mad*. Not like crazy-mad. No, sir. He knew that Slocum was reputed to be a handy man with a weapon, and he figured to take as few chances as possible.

This Sam was another thing entirely. He was younger, for one thing, and that usually meant dumber and greener. If Doolin could knock Slocum off right at the start, those females—hollering "Save us!" and such—would hopefully confuse this Sam Biggle right into an early grave.

All Doolin had to do was figure out how to get close enough to draw a bead on Slocum. Close enough not to miss.

As he mused on this, he just kept following the trail, sure and steady.

Slocum had had an itchy feeling all day.

Not the kind that a man got when there was a beautiful woman clinging to his back all day, putting her hands where they had no business outside the bedroom, and moving them quick every time, like it had been an accident.

Well, that had him itchy too, and he planned to do

something about it tonight. But the other kind of itch had him worried.

He hadn't heard anything, hadn't seen anything, hadn't even got a whiff of anything funny or off the mark, but some sense that he couldn't put a name to told him that he was being followed. Just a feeling.

But he'd learned to trust those feelings when he got them. They were usually right.

So, at about two o'clock, he reined up Swampy and told Mariah to get down. She slithered down his leg like she never wanted to let him go.

Sam, up ahead with Patsy on his paint mare, Tess, stopped too. Slocum would never get used to that horse's blue eyes.

"What's up, Long-Tall?" Sam asked as he helped Patsy slide to the ground too. "We stoppin' again so soon?"

Slocum shook his head, and handed down the bay's lead rope to Mariah. She looked a little breathless, despite having ridden all the way. Slocum bit back a grin. That was something to think about later.

She took the lead rope, but she looked at him questioningly. "Well?" she asked, trying to appear arch.

Playact all you want, Slocum thought. *I may not have figured out why you're putting on this show, but I'm sure as hell going to help you strip out of the costume.*

He said, "You go on up and walk beside Sam."

Her eyebrows hiked indignantly. He didn't think she was putting on this part a bit.

"Walk?" she said.

"Yes, ma'am," he replied with a little tip of his hat, then looked up at Sam again. "Got me a feelin'," he said. "Believe I'll do a little reconnoitering."

Sam's head bobbed. "Got you, Slocum. We'll wander on up here 'bout a half mile, then wait for you."

Slocum nodded, then reined Swampy around. That was one thing you could say for Sam Biggle. He understood about a man's feelings. Course, he didn't always mind 'em too well, last night being a case in point. But he was sympathetic at least.

Course, he was probably going to go a half mile farther, then crawl into the damned bushes with Patsy again.

Well, hell, Slocum couldn't blame him. Slocum had been seeing ghosts and haunts all night and all day. Probably had seen one last night too. He'd likely mistaken a rack of antlers for a rider in the midnight gloom, and it had been a monster of a buck mule deer that had bowled him over.

Most likely.

But then, buck mule deer, no matter how overgrown, didn't light cigarettes.

Or wear saddles whose straps and rigging could rip the flesh off a man's palm.

He retraced the path they had made at a walk, staring out ahead and wondering if he was going crazy. He glanced back over his shoulder just in time to see the others disappear around a wide curve in the canyon floor.

He shook his head.

"I'm gettin' crazy as a goddamn bedbug," he muttered.

But still, he rode on.

Mariah was confused. Also, she was angry. Not at Slocum for dumping her and making her walk, but at Joe. There had been no signal, and she knew he had to be back there.

And then she started thinking that perhaps Joe had

fallen from his horse and was lying back along the trail somewhere, hurt and alone.

She shook her head. That was ridiculous. Joe stuck to a horse like a damned tick.

So what was keeping him?

Doolin Conrad had a feeling too. He hadn't lived to be as old as he had—a free man, outside a jail cell, and with all his arms and legs intact and his neck unstretched—without listening to those feelings. And the minute this one came over him, he rode off the trail and up into the trees that grew thick along both sides of this stretch of the canyon.

He figured he could follow it just as well from above a ways, if a little slower.

Better safe than sorry, though.

Slocum stopped Swampy and sat there, listening.

All the hair stood straight up on his arms, but still, there was no sound except the soft whine of wind through the trees.

He waited.

It had been a good half hour, maybe forty minutes, since he'd turned around. He figured that between Sam and the others going on ahead and the progress he'd made in the opposite direction, he was probably three miles away from them by this time.

He made a decision. He'd ride up into the trees and keep on for another half mile or so. If he hadn't found anybody by that time, well, maybe there was no one to be found. Maybe this time his gut instinct had told him wrong. Maybe he was still just jumpy from last night.

He reined Swampy off the trail and up toward the tree line. He was just making his way around a Mormon tea bush when the impact knocked him flying—straight back, off Swampy, and into the brush.

He heard the report just before he hit the ground, heard Swampy skittering away, and then everything went black.

14

"You hear something?" Mariah asked. She stopped and turned around, applying pressure to the nose of the bay horse she was leading.

"Hear what?" asked Patsy, who had been engaged in conversation with Sam, behind whom she was riding. He was blushing.

"I don't know. Just something," Mariah said. The bay stamped his foreleg impatiently.

From the back of his paint, Sam said, "You're probably just hearin' us. Sound does funny things in these canyons sometimes."

Patsy leaned up to his ear and giggled. Sam ducked his head, and Mariah heard him whisper, "Aw, shucks, Miss Patsy!"

"Oh, never mind," Mariah said impatiently, and began to lead the bay forward again. Maybe she *was* just hearing things. Maybe Sam was right. Maybe it had something to do with the echoing, soaring walls of this long, long canyon. Some of them, seen through the thinning pines and sycamores, were sheer walls of granite or limestone that had become increasingly steep during their morning's travels.

Mariah trudged forward in Sam and Patsy's wake. She hadn't heard another of those odd sounds, but she hadn't heard anything that could possibly be Joe Harper either.

She was more than worried about Joe, although she wouldn't have admitted it to Patsy or Joe himself, for that matter. When the prize was this big, you'd think he'd keep a tighter rein on his girls, check on them every time he thought it was safe.

Of course, maybe he didn't think it was safe.

And maybe he was right. After all, Slocum had just ridden back there to look around, hadn't he?

Mariah pursed her lips. Joe Harper had better hide, that was all she had to say. She had a feeling that you might get the best of Slocum one time, but that was all.

He didn't appear to be a man who'd allow anybody a second chance.

Doolin Conrad rode down close to the body, but he didn't get off his horse.

He just sat there, palms crossed over the saddlehorn, staring at the body.

This one was Slocum, no doubt about it. He was too old to be the younger one, Sam Biggle, and he had a hard-edged, used sort of look about him.

The body lay on its side, so Doolin couldn't exactly see the wound. But he could see a trickle of bloody liquid that had ebbed from the man's chest. That's what blood did when you killed a man—there was a bunch at first, but it stopped when the heart stopped pumping. And by the look of it, this sonofabitch's heart had surely stopped, and in quite a hurry.

He was tempted to get down and have a good search of the body, but he was also aware that his shot could have been heard up the canyon, and he was taking no chances. He didn't much relish the idea of somebody putting a slug into him from the cover of the trees, the way he'd just put one into Slocum.

Slocum's horse had hightailed it up into the trees. Just as well, Doolin thought. He didn't much feel like rounding it up anyway. He had other fish to fry. He figured he could always come on back and search Slocum real good and catch his horse. It was a nice Appaloosa, and looked to be a better mount than the one he himself was riding. Maybe he'd just change horses while he was at it.

And he was thinking about those women up ahead too, if indeed that was what Sam Biggle's passengers turned out to be. Of course, it could be a couple of kids, Doolin thought as he reined his horse around and back up, toward the trees again. That would be just his luck, wouldn't it? Couple'a damned kids.

But if they were women . . .

A smile broke out over his craggy face and stayed there for just a second.

He ducked a low-hanging branch and rode up into the timber, with its cool shadows and pine-needle floor and abundant cover.

Sam and the girls had made themselves sort of a camp. No fire, of course. But Sam had stripped off Tess's saddle and hobbled her so she could graze a mite along with the bay, and Miss Patsy and Miss Mariah had cut a few hard-boiled eggs into slices, all nice and pretty.

Of course, he could have eaten six or eight of those eggs, whole—minus the shells, of course—and single-handed, but he sat like a gentleman and ate what he had.

No sense in taking a chance on getting Patsy riled up or even miffed over something as silly as food. What a woman!

He blushed again, and had to turn away and pretend to be fussing with something on the ground until his face didn't feel hot anymore. Man, just thinking about her and what they'd done last night had gotten him riled up all over again.

And having to ride all morning with her smack up behind him, pressing those big, beautiful titties of hers into his back all the while and talking sweet words into his ear? Why, it had nearly driven him to distraction!

Right this minute, she was sitting so close to him on this rock that their hips touched. By the time they got stopped tonight, his willy was going to be in such a permanent hard-on that he'd qualify for Mr. P. T. Barnum's sideshow.

That is, if he didn't die of blue-ball poisoning first.

Of course, it wasn't like he'd never had a girl before. He'd had lots of women. But the fact that this was a nice girl, and that she seemed to like him so much that she'd just handed over her maidenhood on a silver platter—and the fact that she wasn't anything close to a whore—had him tied up in knots.

Of course, there was her availability too. She was right there, and he figured he could have had her any old time he wanted her. Which naturally was all the time.

He glanced up, and saw Mariah glaring at him.

No, she wasn't glaring, he decided. That was his guilty conscience working. She just didn't have any expression at all. And then she opened her mouth and said, "Another egg, Mr. Biggle?"

"Pleased, ma'am," he said out of habit, and handed her his tin plate. Actually, he could have used a few more than that, but if she was only offering one, that's what he'd take. He didn't want to be on her bad side because, judging from the way she treated Slocum, that wasn't the best place to be.

As Mariah began to slice a freshly shelled egg, Patsy wiggled a little closer to him and yawned.

"Tired, dear?" Mariah asked.

"I could use a nap," Patsy replied, and gave Sam a little squeeze about his middle.

Damn if that didn't stir him up again!

Mariah handed the plate back, the sliced egg arranged on it like yellow and white eyeballs in a ring, all looking up at him, and said, "I believe I'll try to catch a few winks myself. Over there, under that pine would be a nice place." She sniffed. "It has been a trying day, and I assume that our Mr. Slocum is going to take his own sweet time in this casting about for invisible ruffians."

"Don't mean to contradict, ma'am," Sam said, his mouth full of egg, "but if Slocum's worried about somebody creepin' around out there, there's a good chance he's right."

Mariah rolled her eyes. "Pish," she said.

"Yes, ma'am," said Sam, defensive but still polite. "Just the same, I wouldn't wander too awful far from right here to take your nap. Ol' Slocum might scratch you the wrong way, but he's a damn fine man on the trail. Best I've ever seen anyways."

Mariah didn't answer him. She just stood up, whipped her bedroll from the back of Tess's saddle, and without a backward glance, stalked off toward the big pine at the edge of the trees.

"Damn," breathed Sam, "that woman's the touchiest human I've ever see'd!"

Patsy snuggled up so close that he was halfway surprised she wasn't clear inside his clothes with him. "Sam, honey?" she whispered. "Couldn't we go back in the bushes?"

As much as he wanted to just grab her hand and run back there, Sam said, "Now, Patsy, I think I'd best be keepin' an eye out for Slocum."

Patsy's smile turned into a pout. "Oh, but Sam, I'd just love for you to show me some of them other things people do. For instance . . ."

She leaned up and whispered a few things—nasty things, bad things, good things—in his ear, and he forgot all about good old Slocum, back there all alone, hunting for shades and ghosts and mysterious interlopers.

Well, he didn't completely forget Slocum. He did take his rifle along when a giggling Patsy pulled him back into the brush and down behind a juniper bush.

He hurt like hell.

That was the first thing Slocum thought as he rose up through the blackness and into the light. That is, until he tried to move and pain like a hot knife spread out across his chest.

He rolled to his back and felt something wet on his

shirtfront. But he wasn't dead. He was fairly sure of it leastwise.

With a faint groan, he tilted his head up and saw that his shirt was indeed soaked through. Some of it was blood. But . . .

He sniffed the air. Hell, he smelled like a damned distillery.

And then he remembered.

He lay back, dug fingers into his breast pocket, and somewhat painfully, pulled out the flask of whiskey that Jeb Masterson had given him.

There was no whiskey in it now. There was only a round bullet hole through the front, the bullet itself protruding from its back side. That was what had smarted when he pulled it out.

"Sonofabitch," he muttered, and slowly pushed himself up into a sit. He unbuttoned the top of his shirt and took a peek at the damage. Not bad. Only a little flesh wound right below his nipple. The slug had only made it in about a quarter of an inch, and most of the pain that he was feeling was from the alcohol seeping into the wound.

He knew he was going to be good and sore for sometime to come, though. The bruise was already starting to come up.

With difficulty, he managed to get himself to his feet and whistle for Swampy. And while Swampy cautiously wandered out of the trees and down toward him, Slocum checked his watch. Luckily for him, it wasn't busted too.

He'd been unconscious for about a half hour, he figured, and whoever had shot him hadn't bothered to check his pockets. Hadn't even bothered to check and see if he was dead. He was just long gone.

The sonofabitch was probably headed straight for Sam and the women.

Slocum didn't know who this bastard was or what he wanted. At this point, he didn't much care. He just wanted to stop him.

Gingerly, he swung up on Swampy, who wasn't any too thrilled with the day's events so far, and kicked him into a gallop.

15

Doolin Conrad quietly got down off his horse, slipped his rifle from its boot, and made his way down the forested hillside a little.

He took cover behind an outcrop of rock and peered up over the top.

He shook his head. These folks were just making it too easy. Why, it was like shooting carp in a rain barrel! One gal asleep, all by herself across the way under that pine, and the other one down below, rutting like a she-cat in heat with a man he could only suppose was Sam Biggle.

His brothers' other murderer.

He smiled and brought up his rifle.

He took careful aim, right at the center of Sam Biggle's back. Of course Biggle was moving around a lot. The woman must be good, because she was thrashing to beat the band too. She looked like she was enjoying herself.

And both of them naked as jaybirds.

It would be kind of a shame to shoot them right now, he thought. He felt himself getting stiff inside his britches just watching.

But then, there was the late Arvil, Dread, Corbett, and Zeb to think about. They sure weren't much, but it was his duty to exact revenge for their deaths, wasn't it?

"Aw, shit," he muttered, and pulled the trigger.

Mariah woke with a start. She didn't know whether it was the shot or the sound of Patsy's scream, but either one, it did the job. She was on her feet and scrambling into the undergrowth in a slap second.

Patsy continued to scream, a sort of horrible, high-pitched, terrified sound that shook Mariah's back teeth, and she thought, *Joe Harper, you idiot! What the hell do you think you're doing?*

And then she realized that it couldn't have been Joe. Joe was too much of a coward at heart to do something like that, even from behind the cover of trees. Oh, he could take a man's purse or take his life savings with the bat of an eye, but he drew the line at cold-blooded murder.

So if not Joe, then who was it?

And where the hell was Joe?

The sound of Patsy's keening changed, and she appeared, running naked and splashed with blood, from the brush and down the slope of a canyon wall, toward Sam's horse.

Mariah gasped when another shot rang out. Patsy fell and didn't get up.

Hands plastered over her own mouth to hold the scream back, Mariah pressed herself down to the ground, willing herself invisible. There was not a way in the whole world that the sniper could be Joe Harper. And that noise she'd heard earlier? She was suddenly convinced that it had been the sound of Patsy's killer, putting a slug into Slocum.

She had often been mightily scared in the years she'd been running with Joe. More than mightily scared, and more than a few times. But now, as she cowered helplessly in the bushes and saw her companions' murderer step from the brush, Sam Biggle's vest in one hand and a rifle swinging from the other, she knew abject terror for the first time.

"C'mon out, honey!" the man called. He was tallish, with five or six days' growth of stubble on his dark and craggy cheeks. His hair was scraggly, salt-and-pepper, and stuck out from under his stained hat at odd angles. He had a cold, heartless look about him.

Mariah's whimper seeped into her hands, but she said nothing.

"C'mon, baby!" he called again. "I ain't got all day."

He craned his head, looking for her, searching the edge of the trail and the clearing. Mariah thanked God she'd picked the dress she had on. She had only three with her, and if she'd chosen the bright pink one, she'd be dead already. As it was, this one was jonquil-colored, and blended into the yellow-green grass and bushes. She hoped.

"Gonna be a long walk to Carson City if'n you don't come out now," he called.

She pressed herself flatter, if that were possible, into the undergrowth.

Through the tangle of grasses before her face, she watched him take another turn and squint into the weeds directly at her, then shift his eyes to a new location. She relaxed a little, but not much.

He finished his scan of the surrounding countryside, then shrugged his shoulders. He laid the rifle down and started to go through the pockets of Sam's vest. It didn't take him long to find what he was seeking.

The voucher.

Her voucher!

Hers and Patsy's and Joe's, that is.

She watched in maddening silence as he stuffed the paper into his own pocket, threw Sam's vest aside, picked up his rifle, and walked over to the horses. He removed their hobbles, picked up their lead ropes, and started back from whence he'd come.

But just before he disappeared into the trees, he called out, "Last chance, honey!"

He waited a moment, and then, along with Sam's paint and their bay, slipped seamlessly into the cover of pine, sycamore, and aspen.

Doolin Conrad was pleased with himself, all right. Of course, there'd been that gal running off. He would have liked to have taken himself a little pleasure, but it wasn't the end of the world. Besides, she'd never get out of this place alive, not a woman alone, and with no mount.

And even if she did, he'd be long gone from Carson City before she ever straggled into it.

Eight thousand! Hell, he'd never imagined those worthless half brothers of his would be worth eight cents, let alone eight thousand.

But there it was, right on the paper. Payable to the bearer.

Hot damn!

He guessed it was a good thing he hadn't taken the

time to search Slocum back there. Sam and that gal might not have been such easy targets if he'd come along a little later.

Too bad about the blonde, though. Seemed a shame to just leave her lying there, naked and in the dirt.

Oh, well. Easier pickings for the buzzards.

He rode on, leading the paint and the bay behind him. He figured he'd just leave that nice Appy back there. That was a crying shame too, but then, what was one horse in the face of eight grand? And something in him thought it made things more sporting for that lady he'd left back there, the lady that had run off. After all, she might find the damn horse.

Course, chances were quite a bit stronger that she wouldn't come across it. But he figured it gave her a sporting chance.

As he rode down the pass, the paper in his pocket and the spare horses trailing behind him, he began to whistle.

Slocum hadn't heard the shots over the sting of wind in his ears and the swish and clatter of Swampy's rushing hooves, but when he spied Mariah, sitting out in the open and weeping over the naked corpse of Patsy Himmel, he had a pretty good idea what had happened.

She looked up as he approached. She slowly got to her feet and just stood there, looking like a marionette hung up by its strings.

And when he got down off Swampy and went to her and took her into his arms to comfort her, she clung to him.

"It's my fault," she babbled through the tears, "all my fault!"

He rubbed her back. "Where's Sam?" he asked softly, although he had a pretty good idea. Sam's saddle was sitting right there on the ground, but his horse was nowhere to be seen. Neither was the bay.

"I need a blanket," Mariah sniffed. "To cover Patsy. It's not right."

"Mariah," he said again, and gave her a little shake. "Where's Sam?"

She looked up at him, her eyes swollen. "Dead. They're both dead. Where's Joe?"

"Who's Joe?"

She didn't answer. She'd really gone round the bend.

He peeled her off him, and said, "There's a blanket over there, under that pine." When she didn't seem to realize that he'd said anything, he sat her back down in the dirt and set off looking for Sam. There was nothing he could do for Patsy. Her staring, unblinking eyes had told him she was dead before he stepped down off his horse.

He found Sam back in the brush. He was naked too, and shot in the back, but he wasn't dead. Not yet anyway.

"Mariah!" Slocum shouted.

Sam had lost a great deal of blood and was still losing it, and Slocum knew he had to get it stopped as best he could, or the boy would bleed to death.

"Mariah!" he called again, more sternly this time.

She lifted her head a little.

"Sam's still breathin'. Fetch my saddlebags." And when she simply sat there, he shouted, "Now, dammit!"

That seemed to do the trick. She rose and walked to his horse, gathering speed—and what appeared to be her senses—with every step.

"Don't you die on me, you sonofabitch," Slocum said

through clenched teeth as he inspected the wound. It looked too high to have hit the lungs or heart, but then, that all depended on the angle, didn't it?

He turned Sam over gently, and saw that the slug had passed clean through, exiting just below the collarbone. The lead in question had drilled a tiny hole in the ground just below Sam's body, and Slocum dug it out of the dirt with his thumb and forefinger. He tucked it into his pocket.

"You are a lucky bastard," he confided to the unconscious Sam. He thought about dousing the wound with some of that whiskey left in the ruined flask, then decided against it. A splash or two of that would have brought Sam around pretty damn quick, but he would have hollered loud enough to wake the dead.

"Here," Mariah said. She dropped the saddlebags at his side, then knelt down. He hadn't even heard her come up.

While Slocum dug through his pack, she asked softly, "Will he . . . will he . . . ?"

"He'll be fine so long as we get this wound packed good," Slocum said. He pulled out his extra canteen, then tilted Sam on his side. "Here," he said to Mariah. "Hold him steady."

Mariah braced Sam, and Slocum proceeded to wash both the entry and exit wounds. Then he applied ointment to the wounds and packed them. When he didn't have enough bandages, Mariah signaled him to hold Sam while she ripped strips from her petticoat.

By the time he got the last bandage wrapped around Sam's chest and shoulder, the boy was coming to.

"Ouch," was the first thing he said, all long and drawn out and sounding full of gravel. And then he looked up at Slocum, and Slocum's chest—complete with a bullet hole and stained with blood and whiskey—and croaked out, "What in tarnation happened to you, Long-Tall?"

"Shot in the flask," Slocum answered, and when Sam looked at him oddly, he added, "Long story. Tell it to you later."

Sam looked down at himself, then over, up at Mariah. "Slocum!" Sam whispered as he turned bright red. "I'm nekkid!" He slapped a hand down to cover his private parts. "Where's Miss Patsy?" And then he focused on his shoulder and blinked twice. "And I'm goddamn shot! Hell, I *thought* somethin' hurt! Where's the sonofabitch who shot me, Long-Tall?"

Slocum stood up. "You got me on that one, Sam. Mariah?" He signaled with his eyes toward the clearing, and Patsy's body.

"I'll stay with Sam," she said, and scooped up Sam's britches.

"Where's Miss Patsy?" Slocum heard Sam demand again as he walked away, toward the now-blanketed corpse and grave-digging duty.

Mariah's voice floated out to him. "Let's get your trousers on, Sam."

"But—"

"I'll tell you everything as soon as you're decent."

As the sounds of their voices began to fade away in the distance, Slocum pulled a little folding shovel from Sam's pack.

He began to scrape a hole in the dirt.

16

Slocum didn't think to look through Sam's vest pockets until the grave was almost dug. He sat down to catch his breath and take a slug of water, and happened to sit next to a little pile of wadded leather.

But when he checked through it, he wasn't surprised to find the voucher gone. It made sense. It was a perfect day.

And then he began to think about what Mariah had said right after he rode in. "Where's Joe?" or something like that.

He ground his teeth. Something stank, and he figured it was more than his goddamn armpits.

But he got up and finished the grave, dragged poor Patsy into it, and tucked the blanket close around her. Shot right through the heart. She would have died instantly.

At least there was some mercy in that.

He stood up again and started back through the brush, toward Mariah and Sam. Mariah must have told him, because he looked a good bit whiter than his wound would account for.

"Ready," Slocum said curtly. "Somebody want to say some words?"

Mariah helped Sam to his feet and they moved past him. Mariah's only words to Slocum were, "Get out of that shirt and I'll have a look."

It took him a moment to realize it was his wound she was talking about. It hadn't pained him much, not since he'd divested himself of the flask and the alcohol biting it had dried up. He supposed that what with getting shot or knifed or cut up every five minutes or so, he'd developed a kind of wall against pain. All the better.

"Awful shallow, ain't it?" sniffed Sam when he came to the edge of the grave.

"You want to dig it deeper, go ahead," Slocum replied.

"Sorry there, Slocum," Sam said softly.

Slocum shook his head. "No, I'm sorry, Sam. Real worry. This was about as deep as I could get it."

Somewhere up in the trees, a lark began to sing.

"Lord," Mariah began, head down, eyes closed, "we send You the spirit of our sister and Your child, Patricia Mavis Himmel, cut down in the flower of her youth by a heinous fiend. . . ."

The grave was filled in and cairned with stones. Sam sat beside it, his head in his hands, while several yards away, Mariah bandaged Slocum's chest.

"You gentlemen had best keep out of trouble," she muttered. "You get shot up much more, and I won't have any petticoat left when we reach Carson City."

Slocum didn't say anything, and that had her worried. He'd been thinking, and she'd learned quickly that with Slocum, that was a dangerous thing.

Still, her hands were sure as she had cleaned the wound and applied the unguent, and now they were tender but businesslike as she ran the cloth strips across his shoulder and around his chest.

It was much the same bandaging that they had given Sam, but far less bulky and without any packing. Slocum's bleeding had stopped long ago, and the wound was superficial.

"There," Mariah said, and sat back. "You may put your shirt on, Mr. Slocum."

"Just drop it," he said.

She tipped her head quizzically. "Drop your shirt? I'm not even holding it, sir."

"Just drop this Mr. Slocum crud," he growled, and she found she couldn't tear her eyes away from his. She was caught as surely as a deer in an oncoming train's lantern light. "What's your reason for being out here in the first place? Who's Joe? He the one that shot up Sam and me and killed Patsy?"

"No! Joe wouldn't—" Mariah began before she caught herself. Damn it!

"Joe wouldn't what?" Slocum demanded.

She was at the end of her rope, so to speak. Joe was nowhere, absolutely nowhere. Patsy was dead and just barely in the ground. Mariah was alone.

"Kill anybody," she said quietly.

She was hoping that Slocum could be as kind as he could be tough. He hadn't let out a peep while she was bandaging his chest, nor while she'd bandaged his hand yesterday.

"Who's Joe?" he asked. His voice was no less relentless and every bit as insistent.

"I . . . we worked for Joe," she said. There was no reason to pretend anymore. "Joe Harper. He sent us here to waylay you. To steal your money."

Slocum's brow wrinkled as he shrugged into his shirt. "What money?"

"Your reward money," she replied in a small voice. "After you picked it up, that is. We were supposed to gain your trust, let you collect it, and then steal it from you in the hotel in Carson City." She looked down into her lap. "Sorry."

"Well, that's a dumb plan if I ever heard one," said Slocum.

Mariah looked up, blinking and suddenly angry. "A dumb plan? I confess to you, and that's all you have to say? That it was dumb? I'll have you know that my whole, entire future was riding on this! I wanted to get out of here, quit this business and get away from Joe, go back home and settle down, maybe teach school or find a husband. A dumb plan?"

She had risen to her knees by this time, and Slocum, his shirt still hanging open, put his hand on her shoulders and pushed her back down, next to him.

"Jesus," he said, his eyebrows cocked. "Just calm down."

She got herself under control. "Well, it wasn't. Dumb, that is."

Slocum clicked his tongue.

"What?" she demanded.

"Well," he said, buttoning his shirt, "there are lots of better ways you could have done it. Hit us both over the head last night, for instance, then swiped our horses and taken off for Carson. We couldn't have got very far with your bay. You want me to go on?"

She snorted. "Well, it was Joe's plan."

"He still out there?"

"Do you think I'd be telling you all this if I thought he was?"

"I don't know. Would you? This could just be more of Joe's stupid plan."

Mariah ducked her head. She was full of rushing thoughts and emotions, and didn't know which ones to cling to. "He was supposed to signal us. And he hasn't. And once Joe made a plan, the bastard stuck to it for better or worse. I . . . I think he must be dead."

She felt Slocum's big hand take her chin and tilt it up until she was looking at him. He said, "You love this Joe?"

What a strange question! But she answered it truthfully. "No."

"You have any idea who did this?" he asked, nodding toward Patsy's grave and the grieving Sam.

"No. Just a big man." She described him to Slocum in as much detail as she could remember. She hoped Slocum would be kind, although there was not much chance, considering what she and Patsy and Joe had done to him. Many hadn't been kind to her. She remembered that time up in Seattle when Yancy Black took a knife to her face. He would have cut her up good too, if she hadn't kneed him in the balls just as hard as she could and taken off running.

She hoped she wouldn't have to knee Slocum in the balls. She had no idea where to run to, for one thing. For another, Slocum had pretty quick reflexes.

But Slocum just nodded, then helped her to her feet. "All right, Mariah. Gather up our things. Sam?"

Sam's head turned toward them, and he grimaced at the movement. "Yeah."

"I'm hoping this yahoo has got sloppy. After all, he thinks he's murdered us and there's nobody left to chase him except Mariah." He moved toward Swampy and began to check his tack and tighten his girth. "I'm hopin' he's just jogging along real soft."

"You're not goin' to ride after him alone, are you?" Sam asked incredulously.

"Don't see any other horses, do you?"

"But Slocum—"

"Shut up, Sam. Mariah's gatherin' our packs. You and her make camp." He studied on Sam for a moment, then said, "Well, you'd best stay put and watch her make camp. I'll be back. Mariah?"

"Yes, Slocum?" She faced him, her hands full of unused bandages and a canteen.

"That's better."

She tipped her head. "Beg your pardon?"

He swung up on Swampy. "Slocum. Better than Mr. Slocum."

Despite herself, she smiled, just a little.

"After you get things straight, fetch Sam here some laudanum. There's some in my kit. And you two sit tight. I'll be back."

With that, he launched Swampy into a gallop and headed down the canyon. He was soon out of sight, leaving Mariah to simply shake her head.

Sam had stood up, and appeared at her side. "I'll help you with that, ma'am," he said, his voice thin with pain.

"You will not," she replied. "Even your voice sounds all hurt. Here," she added, insinuating herself beneath the crook of his arm. "Come up here, under this tree, and I'll fetch you some laudanum."

"But Miss Mariah—"

"No buts about it. And it's just Mariah."

Five miles ahead, Doolin Conrad was wearying of leading the horses he'd swiped. The bay was really slowing him down. The damn thing had turned out to be lame, and its condition was worsening with every step. Course, he supposed it would've helped if he hadn't loped it all the way.

There wasn't much reason to gallop, though, not even a soft gallop. Hell, there wasn't anybody on his trail. He had more important things to worry about. For instance, what he was going to do with all that money.

He licked his lips. Eight thousand. Man alive! He bet his pappy was turning over in his grave. Not to mention Arvil, Dread, Corbett, and Zeb.

A smile curled his lips.

He was nearly out of the pass. Probably make it out by tomorrow noon, and the rest of the trip to Carson City— and all that money, just waiting for him—was a piece of cake.

Mayhap he'd just leave the country. Go down to Mexico and buy him a big old hacienda and a herd of cows or something. Maybe even marry some comely señorita and have him a passel of kids. Now that would really piss his daddy off, wouldn't it, mixing Mexican into the Conrad blood? Hell, he'd never even let their neighbor, old Boudreaux, onto their property on account of he was partly French. And to his pa, Mexican had meant nigger.

Oh, his goddamn daddy would be ricocheting off the fiery walls of hell, that was for sure!

Doolin laughed out loud and gave his knee a slap for good measure.

He eased the horses to a walk—a good thing, because he noticed that the bay was limping so badly that it was about to go down to its knees.

"Aw, screw you, horse," he said, and pulled out his pistol.

One shot, just behind the eye, and the horse went down. The paint skittered out to the side, and Doolin let loose of him. The spooked mare cantered off into the brush, the lead rope trailing behind her, and Doolin said, "Good riddance."

He moved on at a walk this time, leaving the horse's corpse, still twitching, behind him.

And as he rode, he whistled "Joey Beat the Hangman's Rope." He liked that one.

17

Swampy was tired, but Slocum kept pushing him until he could push him no longer. At least not and live with himself.

He reined the gelding down to a slow jog and kept to the trail.

It was coming on five o'clock, and he knew he didn't have much time until nightfall. He had a feeling he wouldn't be seeing Mariah and Sam tonight.

Damn this sonofabitch, whoever he was! Slocum still had a lingering feeling that it might be this Joe fellow that Mariah had spoken of. Maybe old Joe had had a change of heart about splitting the take with his girls. Con men weren't exactly the most dependable sorts.

He wondered how Mariah had gotten mixed up with Joe in the first place, and then decided it wasn't any of his business. She didn't seem all that upset about his not having shown up, except on strictly business terms. If she was shook, Slocum decided, it had nothing to do with any personal relationship she had with Joe.

And he liked the fact that she'd gotten over that formal

crud. Maybe he'd have a chance to see what she was really like when she wasn't playing a part.

Too bad about that little Patsy gal, though. Even though she hadn't suffered, he felt bad for Sam.

The trail he was following was clear. It was obvious that the man who had made it hadn't given a single thought to covering his tracks, or even trying to. He had stayed right in the center of the long pass where the trail had been beaten wide by a generation of users, taking the easiest route instead of going up into the trees and meandering.

And then, when Slocum was roughly five miles from where he'd left Sam and Mariah—and poor Swampy was about to give out—the trail changed abruptly.

For one thing, there was a dead horse lying right smack in the middle of it. Mariah's bay.

He stopped Swampy and sat there a moment, taking in the stillness of it, and the bullet hole that had cut into the horse's head.

"Sonofabitch," he muttered. It hadn't been a bad little horse. Slocum hated waste, especially a waste of horseflesh.

About ten feet ahead, it looked like this murdering, thieving bastard had turned Tess loose. At least, his tracks went straight ahead, and the riderless paint had taken off, into the trees.

Again, Slocum stopped and worked his mouth around, thinking. He could go hunt up the paint, then take it back to Sam and Mariah, and the three of them could head to Carson together.

Or he could leave the mare for now and go get this peckerwood before he killed anybody else—not to men-

tion cashed in their voucher and made off with their reward money.

He decided on the latter.

At a walk, he rode forward on the tired Swampy.

When the sun dipped toward the horizon, Doolin Conrad
stopped to make camp. He'd walked his horse the last
couple of miles, so there was no need to cool him out.
He just stopped, ground-tied the horse, and set to pulling
down his roll and his saddlebags.

A smile cut raggedly across his stubbled face as he
gathered firewood. He was thinking about the things he'd
planned for that money. He'd decided against Mexico,
that was for sure. Too damn hot, and you never knew
who was going to be in charge of the country from one
week to the next.

He'd thought about Canada—too damned cold—or
maybe about going overseas. He'd decided against that
pretty damn quick too. Too many foreigners, none of
whom spoke enough English to put in a sugar spoon.

No, he had decided he'd go home in triumph, so to
speak. Back to Virginia, where all his kin were dead—
and a good thing too—but where he knew a few people.

And where he could live like a king.

That eight thousand would buy him a damn fine farm
and the folks to work it for him, and he'd still have a
passel of cash left over. Tobacco, that's what he was
thinking about. He'd raise him up some tobacco. There
was money in that.

He'd find him a nice little gal to take to wife, and he
could go back to using his own name. After all, he'd never
killed anybody or stuck anybody up in Virginia. He

guessed there was something to be said for not fouling your own nest after all. It kind of made him proud that he hadn't.

Yessir, Virginia was the place. For the last two miles of trail, he'd been picturing himself strutting around the yard in jodhpurs and a silk vest and with a riding crop, inspecting the staff or the harvest or his kids-to-be. Too bad the South had lost the war. He could have bought a few good breeding niggers too, and raised up his own help instead of paying wages for it.

Oh, well.

He knelt and began to build his fire, pausing to scratch at his rough cheek. There was another thing, he thought. He'd always have a shave. Rich men were always shaved. Always had clean clothes.

And never had to worry about a batch of shit-for-brains brothers turning up to pester them.

Slocum was on foot and walking now. It was nearly dark, but still he crept forward, leading Swampy down the path of least resistance, the path where he was liable to make the least noise.

He moved slowly, one hand soothing the gelding's neck, his ears always alert for sounds from up ahead and his eyes for the signs of a fire's glow.

And at right about the time the sun slipped below the horizon, he spotted it. A tiny flicker up ahead of him.

He halted Swampy and stood there for a moment, watching for it again.

What little breeze there was fluttered the weeds in just the right way, and he saw it again. Just the hint of a flicker. But it was enough.

Quietly, grimly, he mounted Swampy once more and slowly reined him up into the cover of trees.

What was good for the goose was good for the gander, he reasoned.

Mariah put the coffeepot on the fire and began to pull together the fixings for dinner. The sun had just set, and Sam lay silently on the other side of the fire, turned away from her. She had given him laudanum, but not enough to drug him into insensibility. As much as she wanted to talk to somebody about anything, anything at all, she kept silent. Sam would talk when it was time, and not before.

She stewed and fretted about Slocum. She had expected him back by this time.

All right, it had been a silly expectation. After all, he'd probably have a lot of chasing to do before he caught up with Patsy's murderer.

If he caught up with him.

If the murderer didn't catch him first.

She put down a hand and picked up the flask that had saved his life. He'd dropped it next to their pile of possessions, but she'd retrieved it after he'd ridden out.

She turned it over in her hand. A clean, round hole in the fancy side, the side with the gold eagle on it, and the bullet poking halfway out from the other side. Mariah shook her head. Slocum must be the luckiest man alive.

Either that, or the unluckiest. Scars covered his chest, arms, and back, making a patchwork. Scars from bullets, knives, and who knows what. She suspected that one rather long one, which circled his back and swung around his side, had been made by a bullwhip. If there was a

possibility for a fight, she thought, Slocum had surely gotten himself into it.

But he'd lived. That counted for something, didn't it?

Mariah hoped he'd be lucky this time too.

She assembled the ingredients for biscuits and quietly
began to stir them together. Just as she was spooning them
into a skillet to bake on the fire, Sam said, "Mariah?"

He startled her so much that she almost dropped the
batter.

But she recovered, and said, "Yes, Sam?"

"Tell me about Patsy," he said. "I mean, tell me about
her before I met her. Did you know her pretty good?"

She considered this. "I knew her. I don't know that I
knew her well, though. Why dwell on it, Sam? She's
gone. No use digging up the past."

Mariah had meant it to be kind, but instead, Sam suddenly burst into tears. Just as quickly, however, he got
himself stopped and took a rough scrub at his eyes.

"I only wanted to—" he began. "Oh, hell. It just don't
seem fair, Miss Mariah. I mean, Mariah. Her bein' so
young and all, having the whole world in front of her. I
was gonna ask her . . . I mean, never mind. You're busy.
I'm botherin' you."

Mariah sighed. If white lies were ever called for, this
was the time. Although she didn't understand why lying
was suddenly such a great sin. After all, she'd been doing
it for a living for years, now. But there was something
about Sam. . . .

"Patsy was from Iowa," she said softly as she put the
biscuits on to bake and readied the ham for frying. "She
was an only child."

Sam looked up. "No brothers nor sisters?"

"No."

"Must'a been right lonely for her."

"Oh, I think she got along fine," Mariah added, taking care not to meet Sam's eyes. Patsy had been from Iowa, all right, but she'd been raised in an orphanage, her prostitute mother having been killed by a knife-happy customer.

Mariah slid the ham slices into a hot skillet just as Sam asked, "Did she have many gentlemen callers?"

Mariah choked back the laugh that threatened to bark from her throat. Gentlemen callers? "No, Sam," she said at last. At least she wasn't lying. What "callers" Patsy had could in no way, shape, or form be described as gentlemen. "I don't believe so. How are you feeling? Any pain?"

"No, ma'am," he said. "Slocum patched me up real good, and that bug juice you fed me has a right soothin' effect."

"Good," she said, nodding. "Do you think you can eat? Dinner will be ready in a few minutes. It's not much, but—"

Both their heads whipped around at the cry of "Hello the fire!"

Sam reached for his gun. Mariah instinctively pulled back from the fire, knocking the coffeepot over in her haste.

Over its hiss, Sam called, "Who's out there?"

Mariah couldn't see anything but black. And the voice that had hailed them surely wasn't Slocum's.

From the gloom, the voice answered, "I'd appreciate it if I could come in. Name's Orrin McGill, and I done found me a wounded man, left for dead up the pass. I see'd you got a woman in there. I was wonderin' if may-hap she couldn't take a look at him, see if I done him right. Tell you the truth, I got my doubts he'll make it to Carson City."

Mariah gulped.

Sam called, "All right, but come in slow."

18

Slocum, having left Swampy tethered to a tree, made his way silently and slowly through the trees. He crept closer, nearing the glow of the campfire, but always keeping up and away, in the overgrowth.

At last he slid to his knees behind the shield of twin tree trunks, and had a good look at the man he had been chasing.

His brow furrowed. The man was a good bit off, but he looked somewhat familiar. Slocum reached toward his pocket, where he'd stowed his spyglass, and pulled it out.

Shit. He knew the man, all right. His name was David Fisk, or at least that was the name that Slocum had known him by. Of course, that was when they were both working for the Triple D during that range war with Ike Barkly's crew from over at the Crown W, and Slocum hadn't been going by his real name either.

Fisk had sold them out to Barkly and very nearly got them all killed. If it hadn't been for Slocum finding out about the double cross just in time, and for a little quick work by the Triple D's foreman, Slocum and his boys would have been goners.

David Fisk had gotten clean away, and Slocum had been looking for him for five years.

And now he'd found him.

His first instinct was just to raise his rifle, take aim, and blow Fisk to hell.

But he stopped himself. There'd been too many instances of taking the law into his own hands, he supposed. And he could simply wound the bastard and haul him to Carson City. It would probably pain the sonofabitch more to have to go through a trial and wait for the hangman. At least, more than it would if the sonofabitch were to just get shot out here in the middle of nowhere and die right off, never knowing where the bullet had come from.

Or from whose rifle.

Smiling, Slocum collapsed his spyglass and tucked it back into his pocket. He believed he was going to enjoy this—for himself, of course, but for Patsy and Sam too.

He leveled the barrel of his rifle at Fisk and steadied it in the low crotch of the tree. Fisk was sitting quietly by the fire, drinking a cup of coffee, his back turned toward Slocum.

Slocum shook his head. Hell, this was just like shooting fish in a barrel.

He aimed carefully, right of center, up high. He planned to shoot Fisk just the same way Fisk had shot Sam—clean through the shoulder. Maybe he'd get lucky and the bullet would bust Fisk's collarbone too. He didn't mind stoving him up. He just wanted the sonofabitch breathing and fit enough to ride a horse. Or be pulled in a travois.

Fisk leaned forward to pour himself another cup, and

Slocum eased his finger off the trigger. Wait. Just wait.

And then, off to Slocum's right, he heard a sound.

He knew right away that it was Swampy, stamping his foot or tossing his head into some branches, and he cursed the horse under his breath.

Fisk heard it too, and rose to his feet. He stood there for a half a moment, staring out into the darkness, and Slocum held his breath. Fisk had turned, so that Slocum no longer had a clean shot.

He was about to shoot anyway and the hell with hauling Fisk back in, when Fisk sat down again. He gave one last look up the canyon, then picked up his coffee mug.

"Jesus," murmured Slocum.

He leveled the rifle again, took careful aim, and fired.

"Howdy, folks!" said the short, bedraggled fellow who appeared at the edge of their fire's light. He was astride a flea-bitten blue roan mare, and leading a black mule that bore a man across its back, his head dangling.

"Mr. McGill?" said Mariah.

"Oh, just call me Orrin, ma'am, just Orrin," the man said. He was wiry and fine-boned, about fifty, and didn't look to have had a professional haircut in a coon's age. His clothes were patched and ragged and his boots had a few holes in them, but his eyes sparkled in delight at the unexpected company.

Prospector, thought a relieved Sam through the haze of laudanum. Harmless.

"Wonder if I could get down," said Orrin.

"Go ahead, old-timer," replied Sam. "Welcome."

"Many thanks, many thanks," Orrin said, and hopped down off his mare.

Once he hit the ground, Orrin was even smaller than Sam had thought. Maybe five feet six if you stood him on a pile of newspapers. He had to be awful strong, though. He'd gotten that big man up and across the mule, hadn't he?

Sam noticed that Mariah was simply standing there, staring at the wounded man. Funny. He'd figured that the first thing she'd do would be to run over there and have a look-see. But no, she was just standing there like her feet were nailed to the ground.

"Mariah?" he said.

She turned toward him. "Yes," she said, as if she knew what he was about to ask her. "Yes, I'll have a look. Orrin, could you help me?"

"Happy to, ma'am," said the prospector with a little tug on his hat brim.

Sam watched the two of them slide the tall man to the ground, once Orrin undid all the ropes and knots that had held the man stable atop the mule, and watched them drag the unconscious man nearer the fire.

His chest was crisscrossed with dirty bandages and what looked like a spare shirt, tied around him by its sleeves, and his color was milk-white.

And Mariah surely was acting strange! At least, it appeared to Sam that she was. Maybe it was the laudanum, though.

Through a mouth that felt like it was filled with paste, he asked, "Miss Mariah, do you know him or somethin'?"

She nodded. "Yes," she said, as though it were a dire confession. "Yes, I do, Sam. His name is Joe Harper."

Orrin McGill, who was bent over with one ear pressed

to Joe Harper's nose and mouth, cackled and sat up and doffed his hat to the senseless man.

"By crikey!" Orrin exclaimed. "And still breathin' too. Howdy-do there, Mr. Joe Harper! Right pleased to make your acquaintance-ship!"

Carefully, Slocum made his way down the hill toward Fisk's prone body. He'd clipped him just where he'd aimed, but you couldn't be too careful with a varmint like David Fisk, no, sir.

Slocum kept the nose of his rifle, then his handgun, aimed square at Fisk's head. One chance was enough. The second time, Slocum wouldn't be so thoughtful.

He got down to the flat. Still no movement from the body.

He walked over and nudged Fisk with his toe. Nothing. Slocum turned him over.

Well, he was still breathing, all right. And the bullet had come out exactly where Slocum had planned for it to, just beneath Fisk's collarbone.

Slocum was a little disappointed that he was such a good shot.

He disarmed Fisk, patting his pockets and legs. He found, besides two Smith & Wesson handguns, a big old Arkansas toothpick in his boot and a derringer in his back pocket. These he tossed aside.

He dug a length of rope out of Fisk's pack and bound him, hands behind his back, before he even so much as looked at the wound. Or searched for the reward voucher.

He found it in Fisk's breast pocket, and transferred it to his own, poking it down deep with his forefinger.

Fisk tried to come awake while Slocum was treating

him. He growled something or other while the areas were swabbed and treated, and at one time he woke nearly all the way up and studied Slocum's face.

"Morgan?" he breathed at last. "How'd you get up this way?"

"The name's Slocum, you thieving, murdering sonofabitch," Slocum said, but Fisk had lapsed into unconsciousness again, and remained that way for the remainder of the procedure. By the time Slocum had him cleaned up and strapped into a meager bandage, he was still out cold.

And now Slocum had to make a decision. He could stay put till morning, then go back to pick up Mariah and Sam; pick up Mariah and Sam tonight and drag Fisk's worthless carcass along; or go back to get Mariah and Sam tonight and leave Fisk alone here.

He was still mulling it over while he traipsed up the side of the canyon pass and retrieved Swampy. The easiest thing to do would be to hog-tie Fisk, leave him here, and go back alone. But even Fisk deserved better than being eaten alive by some catamount. It was a dilemma.

Slocum shook his head as he tied Swampy next to Fisk's horse. Swampy was tired out, but his time up on the hillside had refreshed him somewhat, and Slocum figured the horse could stand a few miles at a dead walk. That was as fast as Slocum would be able to travel if he chose to go tonight, since there was no light to speak of and he'd be leading a wounded man.

"Aw, crud," Slocum muttered as he poured himself a cup of Fisk's coffee. He looked down at the body. "You're a hell of a lot of trouble, Fisk. Or whatever your name is."

He finished the cup, saddled Fisk's mount and tacked him up, then heaved Fisk's still-unconscious body up and across his saddle. Slocum strapped him in tight. And then he dumped the coffeepot out on the little fire Fisk had made, and kicked at the drowned ashes for good measure.

By the meager light of the stars and the moon, he swung up on Swampy and started back up the canyon, leading Fisk and Fisk's horse behind him.

19

Mariah tore up the last of her petticoat to make clean bandages for Joe Harper. Of all the people in the world!

She wasn't sure just how to feel about the whole thing. After all, she'd just gotten used to him being dead. Just gotten used to feeling clean, after all these years.

And now here he was, in the flesh, groaning nonsensically and rattly-breathed beneath her ministering hands.

By rights, she should have just blocked his nose and mouth and let him die quietly. Although it looked like God was going to take care of that for her. He'd been shot through the lung, and was in pretty bad shape. Actually, she was amazed that he'd survived being heaved up on Orrin's mule, let alone the pack trip down the canyon.

You had to say one thing for old Joe Harper. He was tough.

"Yup, found him nearly out on the flats," Orrin was saying to Sam while he took considerable pleasure in a cup of hot coffee. And in Mariah's dinner. She'd told him she could cook more for herself later.

"Why didn't you just haul him back north, the other way?" Sam asked.

"Hm," said Orrin, pausing. "Well, I reckon 'cause I was goin' this-a-way," he said, and shrugged. "Guess I didn't think about it none. You gonna eat that last piece'a ham, boy?"

"Go ahead."

There was the sound of metal scraping metal as Orrin forked the ham onto his plate. Then he asked, "Sam Biggle, you say? Can't think'a where I heared that name afore. You're too consarned young to own a reputation." He cackled. "So, what you folks doing out here anyhow?"

"On our way to Carson City," Sam answered, and carefully squirmed into a more comfortable position. Poor kid. Mariah felt for him. "And I can think of lots of men who had a reputation when they were young," Sam continued, somewhat indignantly. "Billy the Kid, for one. And how 'bout you? What you doin' out here on the trail?"

"Oh, Carson, goin' to Carson City, all right," Orrin replied. "You mean to tell me that you're up there with the Kid in reputation?"

"Never mind," Sam said wearily.

"You'd better get some rest, Sam," Mariah said, turning toward the campfire.

"Yes'm," Sam replied just a little too quickly. His shoulder must be hurting him quite a bit. "Mariah, you reckon I can take a sip more of that laudanum?"

"Go ahead, Sam," she said, and tied off the last of the bandages around Joe Harper's chest. It would have to hold him.

She started to get up, then thought better of it. She said, "Orrin, have you some rope or twine?"

"Yes'm," he said around a chunk of ham. "Believe I do."

She waited a second, then said, "Would you mind getting it for me?"

Orrin stood up in a hurry, the plate still in his hand. "Oh. Why, sure, sure."

While he rummaged through his pack, she whispered, "Just in case, Joe, old friend."

"Here, ma'am." It was Orrin, handing a length of heavy twine to her. He watched as she proceeded to tie Joe's hands. "You gotta do that, ma'am?" he asked. "The feller seems right quiet to me. He ain't dangerous, is he?"

"Depends on whether you've got something he wants or not," she said, snugging the knot. "Have you a knife?"

Orrin reached into a hip pocket and produced a penknife, which Mariah used to slice away the remaining twine.

"Thank you," she said as she handed it back to him.

"No problem," he replied, but his head was still tilted with curiosity.

"Under control, Mariah?" Sam asked sleepily.

"Go ahead, Sam," she said. "Get some sleep. I'll be all right." She looked up into Orrin's face. "Won't I, Orrin?"

He blinked. "Why, yes'm!" he said, surprised.

Mariah held up a hand to the old miner. She'd be safe, she was certain of it. He helped her to her feet and they both started for the fire. Her stomach was growling.

"You gonna make some of that there supper for yourself?" Orrin asked.

"Definitely," she said.

"Mind makin' a tad extra for me?" Orrin asked sheepishly. "I ain't had women's cookin' in a month'a Sundays."

Only a mile and a quarter after they left Fisk's campsite, Fisk came to.

First it was just a rumbling snort, and then a full-fledged yowl.

"Aw, shut up," growled Slocum. "You'll wake the deer."

Fisk, whose head hung down on the opposite side of his horse from Slocum, said, "Who is it? Why you got me hog-tied?"

"Ain't you gonna ask why I shot you through the chest?" Slocum asked.

"That too," grumbled Fisk. "I ain't never done nothin' to you, friend. I ain't dangerous. Now, untie me and let me ride like a man."

Slocum began to roll a cigarette. "Oh, I don't think I'll be doin' that, Fisk."

"Fisk?" came the reply. From where Slocum sat, it seemed like the words were coming out of Fisk's backside. "Who's Fisk? You got yourself the wrong man, pardner."

Slocum gave a last lick to the quirlie. "That's what they all say."

"All who? Dammit, untie me!"

Slocum flicked a lucifer into life and lit his smoke, then shook out the match. "David Fisk is your name, or at least the name you were goin' by during the Triple D war a few years back."

"Why, you're crazy, stranger!" came the reply. The voice was thick with pain and worry and false bravado.

"I never once went by that name. Where you takin' me anyhow?"

"To see some friends," Slocum answered.

"Friends?"

"Not friends of yours, Fisk. Friends of mine. One of whom you murdered this afternoon, and another of which you tried to."

There was a very long silence, during which Slocum confidently smoked his quirlie and David Fisk most likely wished he'd never been born, or at least that he'd never come to Nevada.

"W-what's your name, mister?" he finally asked.

"Slocum," Slocum answered. "Though you knew me as Pete Morgan when I was up at the Triple D all those years back. What goes around comes around, Fisk."

"Thought I dreamed that," came the barely audible response. "Shit."

And then, more loudly, he said, "My shoulder's bleedin' awful bad."

Slocum just kept on at the same pace. "Must be plumb messy for you."

"I'm not joshing, Slocum. Why, I think I'm gonna bleed to death!"

"Fine by me."

"You are one heartless bastard, Morgan. Or Slocum. Or whoever you want to be this week. Would you stop and staunch my bleedin', goddamn it?"

"Nope. I packed you with enough dirty rags to give you typhoid and scarlet fever and small pox all put together, and I packed you tighter'n a drum. Don't you ever wash out your clothes, Fisk? You're not bleedin' a drop, and don't try to tell me so."

"My name ain't Fisk!"

"What do you want me to call you? Not that it's important. You're gonna hang just the same."

"Hang?" The question came through weakly. Slocum didn't know if it had been the gravity of the word "hang" or if the pain was getting to his captive.

"Yup. For killing a little gal and wounding my friend back where we're headed," Slocum said nonetheless. "And not to mention shootin' me and leavin' me for dead. Shit, Fisk, you are a piece of work, you know that?"

By this time, they had reached Mariah's dead bay, and Slocum made a wide circle around it. Then he stopped the horses and whistled gently, the way he'd heard Sam whistle for Tess these last weeks.

"What you doin'?" snapped Fisk.

"Shut up," explained Slocum.

He whistled again.

This time, a barely heard nicker answered him.

"Good old girl," Slocum said under his breath, then whistled once more.

Tess came down, out of the trees and through the brush, more happy to greet Swampy than Slocum, and whinnied loudly once she saw them. Swampy answered back with a whicker that shook Slocum's bones. Tess came right up, her loud paint coloring flashing in the moonlight, and Slocum snatched up her lead rope without having to dismount.

He tied the rope to Fisk's horse's saddlehorn, figuring that if something should spook Tess, better Fisk's denim-clad ass took the rope burn than his own arm or side.

"You didn't tie that acrost me, did you?" Fisk asked.

"Shut up," Slocum said again, and clucked to the horses.

They rode for perhaps another mile in silence, and Slocum was thinking that Fisk had either passed out or died—he didn't much care which—when Fisk spoke up again.

"My name," he said. "My name ain't Fisk. Never was."

"You gonna say what it is?" Slocum said less than cordially. " 'Cause if you ain't, you might as well shut the hell up again."

"Figure you ought to know. Figure you ought to know why I took them shots at you."

"I'm listening."

"I'm Doolin Conrad," the man said, truthful at last. Or at least, Slocum suspected he was. Only a kin of the Conrad boys would be idiot enough to confess his name in this particular situation.

"Arvil, Dread, Corbett, and Zeb was my half brothers, you murderin' turd."

Only a complete idiot would have called Slocum a turd at that particular juncture, and Slocum did what Doolin Conrad's pa should have done years ago. He snatched up his quirt and lashed Doolin Conrad square across the butt.

"Youch!" hollered Doolin, which spooked the horses.

Slocum had a hell of a time getting them straightened out again. In this, he was in no way aided by his captive, who took to flapping his legs and shouting.

"That'll teach you to mess with me," Doolin snarled.

And that was it. Slocum swung down off Swampy, marched around to the other side of Doolin—the side of the horse that his head was on anyway—grabbed him by the hair, tilted his face up, and slugged him in the jaw just as hard as he could.

Doolin went limp.

Holding the now-unconscious Doolin's head by its lank hair, Slocum said, "When I tell you to shut the hell up, I mean it."

However, on second thought, he did check Doolin's shoulder for signs of bleeding. There were none.

"Thought so," muttered Slocum as he remounted Swampy. "Lyin' sonofabitch."

He clucked to the horses again, and started up the trail.

Mariah had just settled into a fairly good sleep when she heard something curious.

She thought she was dreaming at first, dreaming about little mice, nibbling on clots of cheese and rattling about in the papers stored in her mother's storm cellar.

And then she came up a bit, a little out of the dream, and realized that what she was hearing wasn't part of it at all. Squinting with one eye, she saw that the "mouse" had two legs instead of four, and was rifling through Sam's saddlebags!

"Orrin!" she said, and abruptly sat straight up. "What on earth do you think you're doing!"

20

Orrin whirled around to face her. He brought the saddle-bag with him, for his arm was still deep inside it.

"Holy crud!" he shouted. "Danged if you didn't scare the pee-waddin' outta me!"

Mariah was a bit shaken by his response, but didn't show it. "What are you doing in Sam's saddlebags?" she asked again.

"Lookin' for his medicine," he said, and lowered his voice to a whisper. "He was tossin' and turnin' somethin' awful. Thought maybe a sip of joy-juice would set him right."

Mariah studied Sam. He was snoring peacefully and quietly. "He seems all right to me," she said, one eyebrow arched, and then she flicked her gaze over to Joe. He too was sleeping soundly and, it would seem, comfortably. He'd never been fully conscious since Orrin hauled him in, not once.

Frankly, she didn't much care if he never woke up again.

"Guess he settled back," Orrin said. His hand came up

out of the saddlebag to scratch at his shaggy rat's-nest head, and he laid the saddlebag back where he'd gotten it.

Sheepishly, he said, "Right sorry to fret you, Miss Mariah."

"It's all right, Orrin," she said, and felt herself begin to relax once more. "I'm afraid I'm still jumpy tonight."

He sat down cross-legged, picked up the coffeepot, and peered into it. "Believe there's just about enough for a cup. Care to split her with me?"

Mariah shook her head. "No, you have it," she said, and pulled her blanket more snugly about her.

She'd been running with Joe too long, that was all. Why, even this little old miner had her suspicious. And if anyone ever was trustworthy, it was probably Orrin. He'd brought in Joe, hadn't he? A con man or a thief would have just ridden right by him, would have had more important things to do than waste time helping a wounded man.

Wouldn't he?

She shook her head, as if to shake the thought from it, and at the same time, let out an exasperated little sigh.

"You say somethin', ma'am?" Orrin asked, looking up from his mug, which he'd just poured full.

She rubbed at her face. "No. Nothing."

Orrin took a sip of his coffee, and Mariah thought that by this time, it must have been strong enough to choke a horse. It didn't seem to bother Orrin, though. He pursed his lips thoughtfully and said, "You folks is on your way to Carson City, right? You mind my askin', is you kin to him?" He poked a thumb in Sam's direction.

"No," she said. "We just . . . met up."

"And also, if'n you don't mind, who's . . . who's buried back there?" he went on. "I mean, mayhap it's none of my nevermind, but that pile'a rocks don't look to have been put there natural, and on top of that they look real fresh."

Mariah said, "I'm sorry I didn't explain sooner. It's just that with the wounded men and all . . . That is a young woman. Miss Patsy Himmel. She was my traveling companion."

Orrin's face was suddenly full of sympathy. "I'm right sorry, ma'am, and that's for true. She get shot up, like this boy here?" He nodded toward Sam.

"Yes," she said, staring at her hands.

"Somebody try to rob you or somethin'?" Orrin asked. "Did you murderate him?"

She smiled a bit at his choice of words, and answered, "No. I'm afraid he got away. However, the fourth member of our party has ridden ahead to try to catch him."

Saying it out loud started her worrying about Slocum once more. Where was he?

"Do you have the time?" she asked rather suddenly.

"Yup, I sure do." Orrin dipped grubby fingers into his pocket and pulled out a battered watch. "It'd be right round a quarter to eleven. You worried 'bout that other party?"

Mariah nodded. "A little."

"Been gone long, has he?"

"Since before dark." Mariah stared up the pass. Nothing but darkness.

"Mayhap he ain't comin' back," Orrin said, and there was something in his voice that made her twist toward him.

But he wasn't looking at her. He was looking out, into the darkness.

"What—?" Mariah began.

"Shh!" said Orrin. Smoothly, he pulled his old Winchester from the ground and flicked its buckskin covering away, adopting an expression and stance that were, for the moment, totally at odds with his looks and heretofore eccentric, even comical, behavior.

Suddenly, he looked ten years younger and very serious. Deadly.

But then Slocum's voice carried over the wind. "Mariah? Hello the camp!"

She shouted, "Yes, come in, come in!" and when she turned to look at Orrin again, he was back to normal—stooped, scratching, and sliding his rifle back into its fringed and dingy boot.

Well, perhaps she'd imagined it.

There wasn't time to dwell on Orrin, though, because just then Slocum slowly rode into the circle of light shed by their campfire. He was leading a horse with a body across it. Tess, Sam's mare, trailed behind.

Slocum didn't get down. Rock hard—that was the term she would have used if she were asked to describe him at that moment. He looked like he wouldn't budge an inch either physically or emotionally.

Slocum stared straight at Orrin—with a quick glance over to Joe Harper and back, and said, "What happened, Mariah?"

"This is Mr. Orrin . . . uh . . ." she began.

"McGill," Orrin finished up for her. "Orrin McGill. I found me a hurt feller, and this here lady was kind enough to tend to him. And who have I got the pleasure of addressin'?"

"Name's Slocum," Slocum answered cautiously from atop his horse.

Mariah didn't see why he just didn't climb down and join them. Why he didn't relax and explain what had happened. After all, what threat was Orrin?

The man across the horse groaned feebly and turned his head slightly, and she could see his face. It was Patsy's murderer, all right. Her first reaction was to fetch a rock and beat him to death with it.

She didn't, though.

"Well, pleased to meet you, Slocum," Orrin was saying. "Pleased as punch!" He squinted at Slocum's shirt, at the blood dried on it. "Say, looks like 'bout everybody's stove up around here." He jabbed a thumb toward Doolin Conrad's senseless form. "That one dead too? Sure looks close to it. Miss Mariah here was just tellin' me about the poor little gal what got shot. This the varmint what done it?"

Slocum stepped down off his horse at last, although he didn't take his eyes off Orrin. The fellow looked for all the world like a native species of this area—that being the Gray-Crested Crusty Prospector—but you never could tell who the hell was who, and what he or she wanted.

Not lately, and not in this pass, that was for sure.

"What brings you out this way, Orrin?" he asked coolly.

"Oh, Carson City, Carson City," the old prospector said with a friendly bob of his head and a smile that would have melted butter. "I hear you folks was headed there too. Miss Mariah here tells me you met up on the trail."

Slocum hadn't moved an inch. "That's right," he said. "We did."

"I'd sure appreciate it if'n I could tag along with you for the rest of the way," Orrin went on. "Hell's bells—beggin' your pardon, ma'am. Why, I ain't seen so much carnage in such a short piece of trail since the War of Northern Aggression!"

Slocum relaxed a little. The old mine rat was a fellow Southerner, at least. And he seemed harmless enough—"seemed" being the appropriate word.

Slocum tipped his head toward the stranger's body. "Where'd you find him?"

"Oh, up the trail, up the trail," Orrin said, his head bobbing. "Shot and left for dead. Bet you a silver cartwheel that this fella you got on the back of that horse is the one who shot him up, yessirree! I mean, according to what she done told me."

"It's Joe Harper, Slocum," Mariah said quietly.

He glanced over at her. She didn't look too happy about it. And why should she, after all?

Goddamn it anyway! Here he was, in the middle of the pass, the only fit member—well, fit to skin a Colt anyhow—of a seven-member party, one of which was already shot dead, and at least one of which was at death's door. And by the looks of things, they only had four horses and a mule between them.

Great, just great.

Slocum sighed. "Yeah," he said, leading the horses to the picket line. It was the first time he'd turned his back on the old rock-breaker.

You have to trust somebody, he thought to himself as

he said, "I reckon we'd be glad for your company, old-timer. Your mule too."

He untied Doolin Conrad and let his carcass slip to the ground. The impact was greeted with a low groan from Doolin.

"That'd be fine, just fine," he heard Orrin say as he began to drag Doolin over to the fire, beside Joe Harper.

When he got there, he paused to study Joe Harper's ashen face. For all intents and purposes, he looked like he was dead already save for that little pulse beating in his neck. Forties, Slocum thought. Tall and skinny. He hadn't had time to get much information from Mariah, but she'd told him, in so many words, that Joe Harper was a con man. Didn't look like one. But then, none of the best ones did, did they?

Doolin Conrad didn't look so great either, but by this time, Slocum just didn't give a damn. He left him to lie there, in the dust, without a blanket or so much as a saddle to rest his head on.

Mariah didn't look any too worried about seeing to his comfort either.

"How's Sam?" he asked as he began to strip the tack from Swampy.

"Drunk on laudanum, I think," Mariah answered. She had come up behind him. "Did you have much trouble? With him, I mean." She nodded in Doolin Conrad's direction.

"Nope," said Slocum, hefting his saddle to the ground. "Not once I taught him to shut up when he's told to."

A hint of a smile crept over Mariah's face, then vanished.

"What?" said Slocum.

She shrugged. "I'm sorry, that's all. I know it probably won't do any good, but—"

"Sorry for what?" he asked.

"Sorry about Joe. Sorry about Patsy and Sam and the whole thing."

Now it was Slocum's turn to smile. "You're sorry that Joe got shot up?"

She folded her arms across her chest. "I'm sorry they didn't kill the rat bastard. If he lives, I'm going to leave him so fast it'll make his head spin."

Slocum, fiddling with Tess's rope, paused. "What do you mean, leave him?"

Mariah flushed. "I mean, quit working for him. I didn't mean that he and I, that we, that—"

"Hush," Slocum whispered, and took her in his arms. Her signals had changed quite a good bit since they first met up with her and Patsy, and he figured to take a chance. "You know, Mariah, we've been through quite a bit, considering we've only known each other a day and a half."

She smiled up at him.

"And while I was out there, tracking this sonofabitch, I was only thinkin' about you." It was a lie, but when he said it, he almost believed it himself. God, she was pretty, and she felt solid beneath his hands. Solid and sure and wonderfully curvaceous, and above all, not likely to shoot him in his sleep.

She didn't speak. She just blinked rapidly, as if she were thunderstruck.

He kissed her.

21

Mariah clung to him, molded her body to his, and he welcomed the return of his kiss with even more urgency Apparently, she had been feeling the same things he had, and she was as anxious as he to get things moving and get to the point. His hands wandered over her waist, over her hips, while hers did the same over his body.

And then she pulled away and stepped back.

Breathlessly, she said, "Orrin."

Slocum took a look over Swampy's back. Orrin was hunkered down next to the fire, staring at the sleeping Sam.

Slocum cupped her cheek in his hand. "Go on back to the fire, Mariah. Settle in. I'll be with you soon enough."

She turned her head slightly and softly kissed the palm of his hand. He reached for her, but she darted away, ducking under Swampy's neck. He watched for a moment as she walked to the campfire, smoothing her hair as she went. He watched the swish of her backside, and smiled.

Hell. Lately, nothing was turning out the way it first

169

looked. He didn't mind this about-face on Mariah's part, though. Not at all.

He got on with feeding the horses.

Mariah knelt down beside the fire and picked up the coffeepot. "I suppose we could use a little more," she said, and smiled at Orrin. She hoped the flush had vanished from her cheeks. At least, enough so that Orrin wouldn't notice.

He looked up and said, "Yes'm, that'd be fine. Don't suppose you were gonna heat up any more of that ham?"

She nearly asked him if he had a tapeworm, but nodded instead. "I suppose I can fix two suppers as easily as one," she said, and moved to the other side of the fire. "Hand me that canteen, if you please, Orrin," she added.

He handed it to her, and while she filled the coffeepot with Arbuckle's and water—and wished she had a stray eggshell or a scrape of nutmeg—he said, "That Slocum feller. Reckon he's mighty handy with that gun of his."

"Why do you say that?" she asked absently as she set the pot on a heated rock at the fire's edge. She opened their larder bag again and took out the fixings for biscuits.

"On account of he done poleaxed that feller," Orrin said, pointing toward Doolin Conrad, who was still unconscious. "He looks to be plenty big and plenty mean, that one."

Flour, salt, baking powder . . . "What?" Mariah looked up. "Oh, yes. I suppose that he is. Now that Slocum's with us again, I'm certain we'll make Carson City with no more difficulties." She added a little water, stirred, then added a little more.

"Oh, boy, biscuits!" Orrin licked his lips. "This Slocum. Then he's plenty tough?"

She nodded. "I suppose you could say that." Right now she was more concerned with how he was in bed. It had been so long for her, so long. And Slocum was bound to be a fabulous lover. He was certainly a heavenly kisser.

She dropped the biscuit batter spoon by spoon into a black skillet, plopped the lid on, then set it over by the fire to bake. She found herself wishing that she had honey or jam or butter to make the biscuits better for Slocum. Suddenly, she wanted to make *everything* better for him.

She smiled to herself while she pulled out the ham, and began to slice it into thick, generous, Slocum-sized chunks, thicker than the ones she had cut earlier for herself and Sam and Orrin. There wasn't much left, thanks to Orrin. But they'd be in Carson City tomorrow night. There'd be restaurants and cafés, and civilized people—well, as civilized as they got in mining towns—and there'd be a hotel with mattresses and sheets and soft linens.

How she wanted to lie in a bed again!

And, oh, to lie in a bed with Slocum!

In the beginning, she had dreaded sleeping with Slocum in order to rob him blind. But now, she wanted to sleep with him in the worst way, money or no.

The thought of it made her break out in gooseflesh, and Orrin said, "You cold, Miss Mariah?"

"No," she answered quickly. "No, not cold, Orrin. Not cold at all."

"So you say that fella's name is Doolin Conrad?" Orrin said around a mouthful of biscuit. He shook his head.

"Don't mean nothin' to me, but seems like it means some-thin' to all of you."

That "all" took in Sam as well, for he'd wakened at last, and was currently propped up against a rock.

"I hope to kiss a pig, it does," slurred Sam. Slocum figured that Mariah had gone a little overboard with his bug juice.

Slocum had checked on Joe Harper and Doolin Conrad before he sat down at the fire. Harper still looked more dead than alive and his breathing was ragged and gurgly, but Conrad appeared to be sleeping. Slocum hoped he'd stay that way. He didn't want to waste any of Sam's lau-danum on him—at least, no more than he had to.

He took another bite of ham and biscuit, and washed it down with coffee. It tasted damned good. After all, he hadn't eaten since noontime.

And he watched Mariah. She was a fine-looking woman, and looking better all the time. He had caught her eye just a few moments before, and damned if she didn't blush and duck her head! It was mighty attractive.

At least, his britches were straining at their seams.

He had relaxed a good bit about Orrin. The man seemed to be what he said he was—just a prospector headed for Carson City. He'd told Slocum about finding the vultures circling Joe Harper's body, and how he'd patched him up the best he could, then brought him along. If Harper had had a horse, Orrin said, it was long gone by the time he got there.

Sam was babbling something about Doolin Conrad's family tree. Babbling a good bit more than he should.

Slocum said, "That's enough, Sam." And then he added, "Save your strength."

"Aw, it don't tucker me out to talk, Long-Tall," Sam slurred.

"Well, it tuckers me plenty," Slocum said with a kindly smile. "More coffee, please, Mariah?"

She blushed again, but filled up his cup.

"And me!" Orrin echoed, and Mariah filled his cup too.

"Well," said Orrin, "that's mighty interestin'. About this feller being kin to those scamps the Conrads. Half brother, you say! My goodness. Why, those Conrad boys has terrified half the territory here lately. I heared that they kilt a man and his wife for no more than the fun of it. That was up around Quicksand, or so they say."

"That's right," answered Sam before Slocum could do anything to stop him. "That was my friend, Matt Masterson, and his pretty little wife that they murdered." A tear came to his eye, and he scrubbed at it. "We gave 'em what for, didn't we Slocum? And then this ring-tailed bastard comes round, killin' my little Patsy. . . ."

"Go to sleep, Sam," Slocum said.

Even Mariah seemed a bit nervous. She got up and went to the boy, and helped to ease him down on the ground. "You sleep now, Sam," she said. "You're beginning to talk through your hat."

Sam's brow furrowed. "Ain't doin' no such—"

"Sam?" said Slocum. "Shut up."

But Orrin was fixed on Slocum's face. "You don't mean to tell me!" he gasped. "You two fellers took out the Conrads?" He cackled loudly and slapped his knees. "Well, no wonder this horse's behind is after you! Guess you showed him, didn't you, Slocum?"

Mariah came back around the fire and sat next to Slocum. "He's asleep again. Dozed off right between your 'shut' and your 'up.'"

"Believe I'll do the same, folks," said Orrin with a yawn. "Love to stay up and chew the fat, but morning comes early, yessir, it surely do." He stretched out on his thin blanket, pulled his hat down over his eyes, and within seconds, he was snoring.

Which left Mariah and Slocum.

Slocum threw the last of his coffee from the cup, and it splatted out over the dirt. "Good dinner, Mariah," he said.

She didn't look at him. "A charred boot would have tasted good to you. That is, I mean . . ."

He chuckled. "I know what you meant." He stood up and held down his hand to her. "Come on, honey."

She rose, and when Slocum tipped her chin up, she was flushed and breathing in little gasps.

He smiled and said, "I think we'd best get on with this before you pop."

He didn't have to say it twice. Mariah bent and quickly scooped up her bedding, and then she led him away from the fire, out of its glow, and to a sheltered place in the brush.

He made them a place, and when he turned around, she was already halfway out of her dress. Tentatively, she moved toward him. He cupped her shoulders in his hands and bent to kiss her forehead.

With his thumb, he pushed down the front of her camisole, revealing large, milky breasts with deep salmon nipples. He took one in each hand, and her nipples hardened immediately, tightening, puckering, and darkening.

She was almost panting by this time, and he hadn't

even started. And the level of her excitement had him just about ready to topple over the edge too. Jesus, how long had it been for Mariah?

"Hurry, Slocum," she breathed, and he spent no more time in trying to figure out the situation. He tugged at her dress and her underdrawers, her petticoats having been torn away for bandages, and she stood before him naked. Not only were her breasts beautiful, but her hips were soft and round, her waist tiny enough to be spanned by two hands, and her legs were sleek and nicely turned.

He was out of his clothing in slap time too, and before he knew it, they were on the ground tussling for position. First she was on top, then he, and he finally took hold of her shoulders and said with a grin, "Easy, gal! Let me be in charge for a minute and we'll get this done."

She smiled a little self-consciously but relaxed immediately, and he mounted her. "Now, is this more like what you had in mind?" he asked softly, and entered her.

She was so wet that she was slippery, and driving in deep was like sliding into a warm, welcoming bath. And as he did, Mariah's internal muscles spasmed with an abrupt climax.

Before Slocum could say, "Whoa, gal!" he felt himself being dragged over the edge right along with her.

It must have been some kind of speed record, and he was a little ashamed of himself for giving in to it. But he knew that an appetite like Mariah had wasn't easily quenched. She'd be ready for more pretty damned soon.

He would be too.

He held her close, and after she stopped shaking she kept repeating, "I'm sorry, I'm sorry, I'm sorry. . . ."

He quieted her with a slow kiss, then said, "Seem's like

I have to keep tellin' everybody to shut up tonight."

She smiled then, and he kissed her, deep and long. Her hands went to his cock and began to bring it back to life, stroking, teasing, petting. In no time, he was stiff as a pine plank and ready for a second go-round—hopefully a more leisurely one—when somebody hollered and yelped as if they were being killed.

Slocum rolled off Mariah, yanked his gun from the pile of clothing at their side, and was up on his feet, gun cocked, before he realized who it was doing the bellyaching.

Slocum shook his head. Not only had Doolin Conrad come awake, but he was in pain and complaining something fierce.

"Shit," Slocum muttered, and began to pick up his clothing and climb into it.

"Let me see to him," said Mariah, reaching for her dress.

"No, honey," Slocum said, fastening his belt. "I'll take care of it. Don't move, all right? Don't you move an inch."

She grinned up at him.

He took a step away and then turned back. "Where'd you put the laudanum, Mariah?"

22

t took Slocum longer than he expected to get everybody ettled down.

Quite a bit longer, in fact.

First there was Doolin Conrad, who bellowed like a calf nder the branding iron until Slocum had poured nearly half a bottle of laudanum down his gullet, and offered o slug him in the jaw again. Wisely, Doolin declined the ffer.

However, Slocum tied a gag over Doolin's mouth, just n case.

Orrin had woken, of course, and so there was plenty of oaching.

Slocum was about ready to gag him too.

He checked on Joe Harper, and found that the poor nofabitch had died without ever regaining conscious- ess.

He debated whether to tell Mariah now or in the morn- ag, but it was a decision he didn't have to make. Orrin ollered, at the top of his lungs, "Oh, Miss Mariah! This ller's dead! The one you said as how you knew?"

Orrin's cry woke up Sam too, which was right about a miracle, since even Doolin Conrad's yelps hadn't done that.

Before Slocum knew what was happening, he had a whole burial party waiting on him to dig a grave.

Well, what the hell. At least he had Orrin to help him

By two o'clock in the morning, they had dug the grave three feet down. Slocum figured that was deep enough He climbed out to join Orrin, who had been taking a break at the grave's edge. Slocum sat himself down and started to roll a quirlie.

"We done?" Orrin asked, peering into the hole. "You reckon that's deep enough?"

"It's as deep as it's gonna get," Slocum said as he stuck the quirlie into his mouth, struck a lucifer, and inhaled deeply. He'd worked up a good sweat, but not exactly how he had intended.

The grave was next to Patsy's, although Slocum didn't know how they were going to cover it with a cairn of stones. He'd used up most of the loose rocks in the vicinity to mound over Patsy's grave.

Mariah walked up from the campfire, where she'd been sitting with Sam. She sank down next to Slocum, her hip just touching his, and said, "He's asleep again. I gave him another spoonful of laudanum."

"Good," Slocum said, and took another draw on his smoke.

Mariah gave him a quick look that said she wished Orrin would go to sleep as soundly as Sam had, but then added that she doubted it.

Slocum snorted a laugh.

"Somethin' funny?" Orrin said.

Slocum didn't answer him. He just stood up, and Mariah came with him. "Let's drag him over," was all he said.

He and Orrin brought the body the short distance to the grave site, and Orrin swore a blue streak when he backed into a sticker bush in the darkness. At last they placed the late Joe Harper beside his grave, and held silent while Mariah removed the last of the bonds Orrin had tied him with.

Mariah stood up and tossed the ropes aside as if they were a handful of snakes. "Would you like me to say the words?" she asked softly.

"Go ahead," Slocum replied. He took off his hat and dropped his hands, clasping his wrist before him.

"Dear Lord," Mariah began, and then she stopped. When Slocum looked up at her, she was staring past his right shoulder, a look of stark disbelief on her face.

Slocum started to turn, but Orrin's voice said, from just behind him, "I wouldn't turn around if I was you." There was the *click* of a pistol cocking.

The voice was the same, yet different. There was none of that quaint, rough charm in it now. And it sounded ten years younger. A whole lot tougher too.

"Unbuckle that gunbelt, Slocum," Orrin said. "Real easy. Just one hand, now."

Slocum complied with his left hand out to the side, his hat in it, and all the time he was trying to figure how to get the drop on this joker. He should have known it, should have known that this was probably another jackass after their voucher, just like everybody else. He should have known better than to turn his back on the prospector, and better than to use his almost overpowering yen for Mariah to give him an excuse to relax too soon.

As he slowly unbuckled his rig, he caught Mariah's eye. "How many guns?" he mouthed.

She caught on, thank God, and lifted one finger to scratch the right side of her nose.

He sure hoped that meant one gun in Orrin's right hand.

"Hurry up!" came the barked order from behind him.

Slocum let the gunbelt drop.

"Now kick it in the grave," Orrin ordered.

Grimly, Slocum complied.

"What are you gonna do?" Slocum asked.

"Well, my plans have changed a little," Orrin said. "I was gonna ride drag tomorrow and pick you off, one at a time, like. You first, Slocum. You don't look like the sort a body should give any warning to."

"Thanks," said Slocum. "I think."

"And then I was gonna take that voucher out from wherever you've got it stashed, and leave you folks behind. Oh, I heard the whole story in Quicksand. Real interestin'. Real excitin'. Didn't figure that when I finally came across you I'd find half the population of the territory taggin' along, though."

Slocum said nothing.

"Of course," Orrin said, "I didn't exactly plan to practically ride across old Joe Harper here either. Figures he' go and get himself shot up. He always was a show-off peckerwood," he added in disgust. "That's what showing off'll get you. Shot in the lungs and left for dead. Buried in the exact square middle of nowhere."

"You knew Joe?" Mariah piped up.

"Since before you were born," Orrin replied. "We both worked the riverboats back before the War. But don't try to draw me off the subject at hand, little girl. Slocum, i you want to save me a lot of trouble and yourself being gutshot, you'll hand over that paper now. I know it's got to be on you. It weren't on your young friend over there, and I got a distinct feeling that you took it off Doolin before you brought him back."

"You really are a nasty old fart, Orrin," Slocum growled. "Threatening to gutshoot a man and leave him for dead."

"Nope," came Orrin's voice. "Threatening to gutshoot a man into an open grave, then gutshoot his whore on top of him and bury you all."

Mariah's eyes grew wide. She was terrified.

Slocum said, "You'll make it clean if I give you the paper?"

Mariah whispered a silent, "No!"

"That's what I got in mind," Orrin said.

"Mind if I ask you something first?" Slocum said, mentally calculating the distance between himself and Orrin's voice.

"S'pose not," came the reply. "Just make it quick."

"You were back in Quicksand, weren't you?" Slocum said carefully.

Orrin snorted. "You got that one right, Slocum. You remember a short little fellow, had a beard and a mustache? Cleaning out the spittoons in the bar? Jesus Christ, talk about down on your luck!"

"Can't say as I recall," Slocum said. He lowered his hands—and his hat—slowly, bringing them down in front of him.

"See?" Orrin spat. "Nobody ever does. Even Joe there didn't know me, and I mopped up the floor right next to his goddamn feet. Thought I'd be stuck there forever until you and the kid walked in. Why, you were my dream come true!"

"Glad I was somebody's," Slocum said. Mariah, across from him, was as jumpy as a cat in a room full of rockers. She twitched with nervousness, and her eyes darted back and forth, from Slocum to Orrin and back again.

Slocum took a good grip on his hat.

"All right, hand it over," Orrin said.

Slocum whirled, sinking to his knees at the same time, and batted Orrin's gun hand with his hat just as hard as he could.

The action wasn't enough to knock the gun from Orrin's hand, but it sure as hell surprised him.

Slocum heard Mariah give a little shriek at the same time he slugged Orrin in the gut, then grabbed away the gun as Orrin doubled over.

The gun went off, the slug taking out the limb of a nearby aspen, but Slocum didn't take the time to look. He buffaloed Orrin over the back of his skull with the butt of the pistol, then knocked him all the way to the ground and sat on him.

He heard a little whoosh as all the air went out of Orrin.

"I've had just about enough of this crud to last me a lifetime," he muttered before he turned toward Mariah. She was standing stock-still, both hands covering her mouth, her eyes big as saucers.

"Honey," he said, "you wanna find me some rope or something?"

It took her a second, but she moved.

An hour and a half later, Joe Harper's grave was filled in, Orrin was hog-tied on the back of his roan, Doolin Conrad

was trussed and slung over Orrin's mule and babbling in
his drug-induced sleep, and Slocum woke up Sam.

It wasn't easy.

At last, he came around. He blinked slowly, taking in
the scene around him, then taking in the new grave. He
gave one last look at Orrin, seated atop that mule and
looking daggers at just about everybody.

Sam drawled, "I miss somethin', Long-Tall?"

Slocum nodded. "Guess you could say that, Sam.
C'mon, get up. We're movin'."

"It's still dark!" Sam argued, and took a rub at his eyes.

"Not for long," said Mariah, holding out a cup of hot
coffee for him. "It'll be dawn in a couple of hours, give
or take."

Sam took the steaming mug. "Don't see why I couldn't
sleep in. I'm a wounded man."

"A wounded man who needs to see a doctor," Mariah
said sternly. "In Carson City. Now, drink up or we'll leave
you."

Sam sighed. "You're gettin' as bad as ol' Slocum here.
Hoop-de-doodle!"

The party made its way to Carson City, arriving the next
evening without further incident, other than a lot of flut-
tering lashes and wistful sighs on Mariah's part, and a
whole lot of telling himself to take it easy on Slocum's
part.

The bank was closed, although the sheriff's office was
open, and Slocum and Sam stopped by to announce their
presence, show their voucher, and drop off the prisoners.

"By gosh and by golly!" exclaimed Sheriff Jamison as
he pumped their arms. "Glad to make your acquaintance,

fellers! Them Conrads was just too vile to live."

"Got another one for you out here," Slocum said. "Conrad, that is."

Jamison's brows shot up. "Another one?"

"Doolin Conrad," Slocum said. "Goes by a passel of names. You might want to go through some back posters. I reckon he's wanted for murder in the Triple D range wars. Plus he killed a cute little gal a couple days ago. I'll give you the rest of it tomorrow, if you don't mind. I'm plumb tuckered."

"The sonofabitch'll hang for killin' my Patsy," Sam grumbled, then said, "And we brought in a holdup artist, calls himself Orrin Somethin'-or-Other."

"I'll be damned," the sheriff said, and scratched the back of his head. "You boys gone in the law business all of a sudden?"

"No," replied Slocum wearily. "Tryin' to get away from it, as a matter of fact."

Jamison put his hat on and peered out the window. "And who's the gal out there? Another outlaw you want I should lock up?"

Slocum felt Sam's gaze on the back of his neck.

"Nope," Slocum answered quickly. "Just a lost pilgrim."

When he turned, Sam had visibly relaxed.

The three travelers went on up to the hotel then, dropping Sam at the doctor's place next door, and Slocum registered for them all.

"Give this to the tall, skinny feller with the bandaged shoulder when he comes in," Slocum said, flipping the second key back at the clerk. "Tell him to sleep in as long as he likes. And not to bother us."

He tucked Mariah under his arm, and up the steps they went.

"Thank you for not turning me in," she said after he'd locked the door behind them.

"Now, why would I want to do a thing like that?" He grinned. He threw his hat onto the bedpost.

Mariah shrugged.

He took her in his arms. "How about a little love-makin'?" he whispered, then grinned again. "Only slower this time. And the next. And the next."

She smiled up at him, all soft and melty. "It would be my distinct pleasure, Mr. Slocum. As if I haven't been waiting all day. And all last night too!"

He chuckled in the dim light. "What you gonna do tomorrow?" he asked softly as he began to unbutton her dress.

"Look for work?" she said. Her fingers were busy with his belt.

"Oh, I think you oughta go back East," he said, and eased the dress from her shoulders. "That's what you really want, isn't it?"

She paused. "Don't tease me, Slocum."

"Not teasing you, honey. How'd you like two thousand? Stake money, kind of. It ought to get you back home and set you up fine."

She stared at him for the longest time, and then she said, "You're not joshing me, are you?"

"I never josh about money," he said with a shake of his head. "Hell, I'd just waste it anyhow. Gonna let the kid take half, and give you half of my half. A couple of thousand is all I need. More than I need."

Mariah began to cry.

Slocum pulled her close and held her. "Honey?" he said after a minute. "Mariah, honey?"

Sniffing, she looked up at him. "Yes, Slocum?"

"I'm about to bust."

She smiled and pulled his belt from its loops. "Let me take care of that for you, darlin'. It would be my most gratifying pleasure."

Watch for

SLOCUM AND THE BITTERROOT BELLE

292nd novel in the exciting SLOCUM series
from Jove

Coming in June!